The Runaways

By Kristin Butcher

Kids Can Press

Kids Can Press acknowledges the financial support of the Ontario Arts Council,
the Canada Council for the Arts and the Government of Canada, through the
BPIDP, for our publishing activity.

Published in Canada by
Kids Can Press Ltd.
29 Birch Avenue
Toronto, ON M4V 1E2

Published in the U.S. by
Kids Can Press Ltd.
2250 Military Road
Tonawanda, NY 14150

www.kidscanpress.com

Edited by Charis Wahl
Interior designed by Tom Dart/First Folio Resource Group, Inc.
Printed and bound in Canada

CM 97 0 9 8 7 6 5 4 3 2 1
CM PA 97 0 9 8 7 6 5 4 3 2

National Library of Canada Cataloguing in Publication Data

Butcher, Kristin
     The runaways

ISBN 1-55074-413-5 (bound)
ISBN 1-55074-379-1 (pbk.)

I. Title.

PS8553.U6972R86 1997   jC813'.54   C97-930877-1
PZ7.B87Ru 1997

Kids Can Press is a Nelvana company

For Sara, who never lets me quit

CHAPTER I

NICK DIDN'T KNOW IF HIS CHEST ACHED BECAUSE HIS lungs were bursting or because his heart was breaking. All he knew for sure was that he had to keep running.

He'd covered the three blocks down Falcetta Boulevard to Ramsey Avenue before he realized he was heading for home. It was a natural instinct, but it was wrong. Angry at his own stupidity, Nick changed course at the next intersection. And the next. He knew they weren't following him, but he kept running, hearing only the blood pounding in his ears. It was dark now and there were few cars or people on the streets, but Nick hardly noticed – he was concentrating on the rhythm of his breathing. He couldn't let himself feel the ache growing in his side – that would suck away the last of his hope, and he wouldn't be able to run another step. Then he would *have* to go back.

As he turned the corner at Kelly Lane and Kirkland Avenue, he looked back — just in case they were following. It was a mistake.

Slam! He crashed hard into what felt like a wall. Then he reeled, unable to get his balance. His backpack tore free of his grip and flew off into the night. He stumbled over something — metal, he thought — that gouged his shins and sent him crashing to the ground.

Woomph! As the full weight of his body hit the sidewalk, the air rushed from his lungs. For several seconds he lay winded, gasping like a fish out of water.

Once he got his breath back, he didn't have the will to run again. But common sense told him he couldn't lie sprawled on the sidewalk. Gingerly, he tested the various parts of his body. He was bruised and scraped and sore, but nothing seemed to be broken. As he started to push himself to his feet, he heard a groan.

There it was again. It wasn't a wall he'd slammed into, but a person.

He struggled to his feet and stumbled in the direction of the sound, through the crazy shadows cast by the streetlights. Nick didn't see him right away because, in the collision, the man had been thrown from the sidewalk into a bush against a fence. That's where he was sitting, as though the bush was an overstuffed chair.

Except that the man was stuck, Nick realized. His feet, one shoeless, weren't touching the ground, and his muddy brown overcoat was spread wide, snagged here and there on the sharp branches of the bush. The worst part though, Nick discovered as he tried to free the man from his prickly throne, was the man's head. His hair, a shoulder-length mane of silver, had become tangled in the bush, and every time he tried to move his head, his hair tugged at his scalp, causing him to wince in pain.

"Hold still," Nick urged. "Let me untangle you." But it was an impossible job, especially in the dark. Finally, Nick snapped the tangled twigs from the bush. They were still caught in the man's hair, but at least he was free.

"Are you okay?" Nick asked, helping the man to his feet.

"Hmmph," the man grunted. "No thanks to you. Why don't you watch where you're going? You could've killed me, you crazy kid. Where's my shoe?" He shrugged Nick's hand from his arm and began searching the ground.

Feeling guilty and not knowing what else to do to make up for the accident, Nick joined in. The shoe had landed on the grass near the curb, right next to Nick's backpack. He ran to retrieve it. It was old and scuffed, but Nick knew it had once been a quality shoe. He'd seen ones like it in Cole's closet, and Cole always had the best. The sole of the shoe was worn thin. In one place it had given out altogether and a piece of cardboard had been stuck inside to cover a hole about the size of a quarter. The shoe had no laces. No wonder it had flown off the man's foot, Nick thought.

As Nick started back with the shoe, he studied the man, who had shuffled back onto the sidewalk and was waiting impatiently under a streetlight. He was short and old. His bushy eyebrows, long thick hair, and even the stubble on his chin were silver. His face was lined and leathery. He looked like a fisherman who had spent his life in the salt spray and sea wind. Whoever he was, he'd seen better days. His long threadbare coat was a couple of sizes too big and the sleeves hung down over the man's knuckles. The bottoms of his trousers were ragged and a big toe poked through the sock on his shoeless foot.

Yet despite his scruffy appearance, the man carried himself with a dignity that Nick found surprising in a bum. But a bum was what he was. Nick realized that he had seen him many times, wandering the streets, digging through trash for bottles and pop cans, placing them carefully in the two-wheeled wire shopping cart he always pulled behind him. He was as much a part of Andersonville's identity as the clock in the city hall tower.

Everybody knew him – at least to see him. His

name was Luther. Nick knew he must have a last name too, but no one seemed to know – or care – what it was. Nick wondered about that. If you didn't have an address, maybe you didn't need a last name either. Nick tried to imagine it – no home, no name.

"What're you staring at?" Luther's hard black eyes glared at Nick from beneath angry eyebrows. He snatched his shoe out of Nick's hand and returned it to his foot. Then he took a few experimental steps, as though he were trying on new shoes at a store. "Hmmph!" was all he said, glaring again at Nick.

"Let me help you get the twigs out of your hair."

Luther raised an arm to fend off Nick's help and backed up, placing his cart strategically between them.

"Don't you think you've done enough already?" he barked.

"But I just want to help. I'm really sorry. This was all my fault, and I want to make sure you're okay. You *are* okay, aren't you?" Nick finished hopefully.

"*You* are *okay, aren't you?*" Luther mimicked in a high-pitched whine. "What do you care? Mind your own business. Can't a man even take an evening stroll without being mowed down by some thoughtless kid? What are you doing racing around the streets after dark anyway? Don't you have a home?"

"I-I-I ..." All the horrible events of the day stampeded through Nick's brain and panicked him. He might be better dressed than Luther, but he was no better off. *No*, he thought, *he didn't have a home, not anymore.*

Nick turned and ran.

CHAPTER II

THE BUS STOP APPEARED JUST WHEN NICK HAD admitted to himself that he couldn't run any farther. Exhausted, he slid onto the bench. There was no one else at the bus stop, so he didn't even try to stop the tears from rolling down his cheeks. He had to let them out or he would burst from pain – the pain of his mother and Cole and his whole mixed-up life.

If he could just turn time back two years, everything would be perfect. Two years ago, when Nick had been ten, life had been great – just him and his mother. His parents had separated before Nick was born; his mother said that things just hadn't worked out. Sometimes Nick wondered exactly what hadn't worked, but his life was so full of friends, school and sports that there wasn't much room for a father he'd never known, and his curiosity never lasted long.

Besides, his mother was better than ten dads. She could throw a football, hit a baseball and tie up skates. She wasn't afraid of snakes or frogs, and she liked camping. She could whistle through her fingers, climb trees and change the oil in her car. Nick would have matched his mother against anyone else's dad.

But she was his mom, too. Even when she was covered with grease from fixing a pipe under the kitchen sink, she still had that fresh-cut flower smell. She came home from teaching high school with a briefcase full of marking every night, but she still found time to bake the best chocolate chip cookies in Andersonville.

She was always there when Nick needed her. When he had fallen off the play structure at school and broken his arm, his mom had driven him to the clinic. When he had had to have his tonsils out, his mom had stayed with him at the hospital the whole time. When he hadn't made the baseball team, she had practiced with him and helped him to believe he'd make it the next time. And he had.

With a mom like his, Nick never missed having a father. In fact, he never wanted a father. He had his mom and she had him. And that was all they'd needed.

Until Cole came along. That's when everything had changed. Cole was an editor for *The Andersonville Times*, the town newspaper. Nick's mother had met him when she'd taken one of her classes there on a field trip. They had been dating for two months before Nick even knew Cole existed. Nick had felt betrayed – why was she seeing this guy? She'd never gone on dates before that Nick could remember. Why did she have to start now?

Naturally, Nick hated Cole and didn't even try to hide his feelings. There was no sense encouraging the man – the sooner he got out of Nick's life, the better.

But he didn't get out. As the weeks and months passed, Cole was at their house for supper several times a week and stayed after Nick had gone to bed. When he wasn't hanging around, he was calling to invite Nick's mother to a movie or dinner or to go dancing. The more Nick saw of Cole, the less he saw of his mother.

It wasn't fair, and he told his mother so. The silly smile she'd been wearing for months was instantly wiped off her face. Then things got worse – they began including Nick in their outings. Picnics, bike rides, football games, movies – it was unbearable.

Nick started doing his homework in his room so he wouldn't be tortured by Cole trying to help him. He stopped answering the phone and the door just in case it was Cole. When he played baseball, Nick no longer looked for a reassuring wave from his mother, because he knew Cole would be glued to her side, smiling his *I'm-really-not-a-bad-guy* smile and giving Nick a thumbs-up.

"Nick," his mother said one day when he had become so hostile she couldn't ignore it any longer. "This behavior has to stop."

"What behavior?"

"You know darn well what behavior – your sulky rudeness toward Cole. It's humiliating. I won't put up with it."

"And I won't put up with *him*!" Nick blurted. "I don't like him! I *hate* him!"

"You don't hate him," his mother replied calmly. "You don't even know him. He's a wonderful person, Nick, and you'd like him if you'd just give him a chance. He likes *you* very much and …"

"Yeah, right! He's pretending he likes me because I'm your kid! Why'd he have to come and spoil everything?" Nick was shouting. "We were just fine before *he* came along! Why'd you let him mess us up? Why'd you have to get a boyfriend anyway? Don't you love me anymore?"

His mother gasped. She reached for Nick, but he pulled away.

"Please, Nick."

"Leave me alone. If you really loved me, you'd get rid of Cole. Then we could be like we used to be."

His mother's eyes were shiny with tears. "Nick, I will always love you. You are my son and a mother's love for her child is unbreakable. I always want to be a part of your life, and you'll always be a part of mine. But that doesn't mean we don't have room for others."

Now Nick was crying.

"But why Cole? Why him? Why now? Couldn't we just get a dog?"

At that, they couldn't help it – they both started to laugh through their tears.

"When you get older, Nick, you'll understand. But for now you're just going to have to trust me. Cole isn't your enemy. He's a wonderful person. He's thoughtful and generous and intelligent and fun. I've never met anyone quite like him. He makes me happy. I know you'll like him too. You only have to give him a chance."

"But you never needed anyone else before."

His mother shrugged. "Nick, I didn't go looking for someone. It just happened." There was a pause. "I really need you to try, Nick. Please?"

So Nick had tried. He learned to tolerate Cole and, when the inevitable happened, Nick accepted their marriage. But it was hard getting used to having Cole around all the time. Nick resented the little things the most – Cole's toothbrush, Cole's dirty clothes in the hamper, telephone calls – really personal, permanent things. He didn't like them, but he had learned to live with them. This last thing, though, was too much.

A bus pulled up to the stop and two women got off. Self-consciously, Nick swiped at his wet cheeks with his jacket sleeve.

"Which bus are you waiting for, son?" the bus driver called out the open door.

Nick was startled.

"Pardon me?"

"It's pretty late for you to be out. I was wondering which bus you were waiting for?"

Nick didn't know the buses at this stop, so he said, "I'm not waiting for a bus. I'm waiting for my mom. She said she'd pick me up here. She should be here any minute."

"Okay, then," the driver smiled and shut the door.

Maybe he *should* take a bus, Nick thought as he watched the bus pull away. He had the fare. But which one would he take? Where would he go? He shivered and zipped up his jacket. The day had been warm for late September, but it was cooling off quickly. Nick shivered again. What was he going to do? He couldn't just sit at this bus stop all night.

Nick stared across Kirkland Avenue at the hill. It was haunted – everyone said so. Nick had only been on Old Hill Road once, when the guys had dared him to run from one end to the other. It was about a quarter of a mile long and barely wide enough for a car. Its pavement was crumbling and riddled with potholes. It ran like a horseshoe around the wooded hill, both ends joining Kirkland Avenue, the six-lane highway that connected the center of Andersonville with Route 16. Over the years, Old Hill Road had become overgrown, but since it didn't go anywhere, the citizens of Andersonville were content to let the hill reclaim it.

The base of the hill facing Kirkland Avenue was ten feet of rock, cut sheer when the highway was built. The flatness of the rock made it impossible to climb but perfect for graffiti, and there was always some slogan or message in fluorescent paint. *Scott loves Allison* and *Ban Animal Testing* had been there for a while. Above the rock face, the hill was so thick with trees and bushes that Nick couldn't see the McIntyre mansion at all.

Not that it mattered. No one lived there now — unless there were ghosts, of course. When Andersonville had been new, the McIntyres had built that huge house on top of the hill. They had owned the first store, McIntyre's Mercantile, and the first hotel, The Empire. The town had grown out of the gold rush and been named after the first miner to strike it rich, but it had prospered because of the McIntyres. For three generations they had lived in that house on top of the hill. Kristina McIntyre had been the last. She'd never married, and when she died the town had boarded up the house and let it be. People said the McIntyre ghosts were there still, in their house on the hill, looking out over Andersonville.

If they were, at least they'd be friendly, Nick decided. He picked up his backpack, checked for cars and ran across the highway.

CHAPTER III

OLD HILL ROAD WAS MUCH DARKER THAN NICK had expected. The streetlights didn't penetrate the trees, and Nick wasn't more than ten steps into the woods before he could no longer see where he was going. The only other time he'd been on Old Hill Road it had been broad daylight. Nick stumbled over the rutted road, feeling his way along the bushes. Anything could be hiding in these woods – wild animals, thieves, even murderers! He could hardly hear the traffic from the highway, and there was only a thick canopy of trees where the sky should have been.

A nearby bush rustled. Nick jumped. He wasn't alone after all. Strain his eyes as he might, he could see nothing in the darkness. He told himself he was being silly – it was probably just a snake or a mouse – but he hurried on as quickly and quietly as he could.

Nick stumbled into something blocking the road. He ran his hands over it to find rough, pointed wooden slats. Something brittle flaked off in his hands. Paint, probably. It was a fence – no, a gate – he realized, shuffling around it. He must be at the entrance to the McIntyre mansion. He squinted toward where he figured it must be, but his eyes were useless. The darkness was like a heavy, wet blanket.

Were the McIntyre ghosts watching him fumble his way toward their home? Were they walking beside him? Suddenly he wasn't so sure about their friendliness. Maybe they were angry that he was trespassing. Maybe they were going to throw him off their hill, out of their woods. Maybe they were going to …

Nick tried to swallow, but he couldn't. He forced himself to concentrate on picking his way toward the house. His feet found a stone walkway and he felt the path begin to rise. After about ten cautious steps, he bumped into some stairs. Without his eyes to guide him, he was nervous about climbing the stairs. Judging from the height of the McIntyre place above Kirkland Avenue, there must be a lot of them. What if he got part way up and lost his balance? He shivered at the thought. Still, he'd come this far … All the same, he wished he had a flashlight.

He slipped his arms through the straps of his backpack to free his hands. Then he bent down and felt along the first step. He judged it was about six feet long and, like the pathway, made of stone. Well, he might fall *off* the stairs, he decided, but he wouldn't fall *through* them. Nick slowly began to climb on all fours, planting his hands and feet firmly. He counted as he climbed. At thirty-five, he sat down to rest and wondered if the stairs went on forever. He thought about going back, but climbing down the stairs in the dark would be even more frightening than going up them.

Nick was cold and tired. He found himself wishing he was back home, safely tucked into his own bed. Then he remembered why he'd run away. He began to climb again with determination. At sixty, the stairs stopped and the ground levelled off. The stone walkway began again and Nick followed it a short distance until he felt another stairway ahead of him. This one was wooden. Nick took a deep breath. He had a feeling he had reached the house.

He wished he could see it. The handrail and steps were slabs, as thick and solid as concrete. At the top of the stairs was a landing. That must be the porch.

Nick wasn't sure what to do next. What if he couldn't get in? He hadn't thought of that before. The windows and doors would probably be boarded up, and he had no way of prying them open. With arms stretched in front of him, he inched his way forward. His hands met something rough – brick. He stepped to his right, running his hands along the brick as he went, until he felt wood. It was a window frame and, as Nick had feared, it was boarded up. He pulled on one of the boards, but it wouldn't budge. Nick shuffled back the way he had come, and then went on a bit farther. There should be a door somewhere near the top of the stairs. There was, but it too was boarded over. If he couldn't get in, he would have to sleep on the porch.

He tugged on a board about chest high. It was nailed tight. Then he tried one that was level with his waist. To his surprise, the end of the board came away easily and, caught off balance, Nick stumbled backward. Excitedly, he felt for the next board down. It too pulled away easily. As did the next one. And the next one. He was going to get in *unless* ...

From somewhere in the darkness an owl hooted, and Nick jumped.

...unless the door was locked. It should be. Nick reached his hand around the loosened boards and under those still nailed fast. He found the handle – cold metal with a thumb lever at the top. He pressed the lever. Nothing. He reached in with his other hand and pressed hard with both thumbs. There was a click and the creak of ancient hinges as Nick pushed on the door. It opened.

Cautiously, he stepped around the boards he had pried loose and ducked under the ones blocking the top half of the entrance. He was inside the mansion, as though he had just advanced to a new level in a video game. The door groaned again as he pushed it shut, and he gritted his teeth at the sound.

He was suddenly exhausted – his run, his collision with Luther, his blind climb to the house, the cold of the night and the fear of the unknown had all taken their toll. He felt his way along the hallway and around a corner into a room. He slipped off his backpack and slid down the wall to the floor. Using the backpack as a pillow, Nick curled into a ball, huddled against the night's chill. Too weary to control his mind, his thoughts drifted.

"Let him go," Cole had said as Nick had bolted out of the restaurant after they had dropped their bombshell.

And Nick's mother *had* let him go. That proved it – he obviously didn't mean anything to her anymore. Not now that she had Cole. And now that *she was going to have a baby*!

But Nick was too tired even for his misery to keep him awake, and he was fast asleep before his tears reached his chin. So he didn't hear the front door creak again, and he didn't hear the footsteps in the hall.

CHAPTER IV

W HEN NICK AWOKE, HE THOUGHT IT MUST BE THE middle of the night because it was still dark. But this darkness wasn't as suffocating as when he'd climbed the hill. It was softer, paler, more watered down. In this darkness, he could see.

He peered around him. The room was small and square and empty. It had a high ceiling and papered walls. Across from him was a window, narrow and high, stretching the length of the wall. It had been boarded over, but chinks of light appeared through the cracks, and Nick knew it was day.

He decided to explore. If the ghosts hadn't attacked him in the night, he doubted that they would bother with him now.

Though the light was dim, Nick had no trouble seeing his way. The house was the largest he had ever been in. Each room seemed to grow out of the one before it, and Nick completed a circle of the entire first floor without returning to the main hallway. Some of the rooms were huge, others were barely larger than closets. Without any furniture, it was impossible for Nick to tell what they had all been used for, but he did recognize the kitchen – a large room with three smaller rooms off it. Nick saw cupboards, a stove and sinks, though they were nothing like the ones at home.

Back in the main hall, Nick hesitated before starting up the curved, elegant stairway that led to the second floor. He wanted to see the outside of the house first. He needed to see the hill, to experience with his eyes the climb he had made in the dark.

The front door was solid, heavy oak. Its hinges protested Nick's tugging, though less loudly than they had in the night. The daylight entered reluctantly, as if unsure of its welcome. Nick ducked under the boards blocking the doorway and stood on the porch.

The sky was leaden, heavy with thunderclouds, and Nick could smell rain coming. Where the sky ended, the trees began, an endless blur of russets, yellows, oranges and reds.

Nick looked toward the stairs. Sixty of them, he recalled! Sixty stone steps tangled with weeds and slippery with moss. He wondered how he had ever climbed them at all, never mind in the dark. And at the very bottom, still open to the road, was the gate, toy-sized from this height. Nick had intended to go down the stairs to view the house from a distance, but he changed his mind. He wasn't going to confront those stairs again if he didn't have to.

Instead, he'd explore the second floor.

With each step up the grand staircase, the house seemed to get brighter. When Nick reached the second floor landing, he realized why. The windows on this level hadn't been boarded up. He hurried into one of the rooms and peered anxiously out its window. The glass was dirty inside and out, and trees blocked most of his view, but Nick saw what he was looking for. There, far below him, with miniature cars zipping up and down, was Kirkland Avenue. He felt the tension drain from his body – it was a relief to see something familiar. He could see the bus stop, where he had sat just hours ago, crowded now with people on their way downtown. Beyond lay the familiar landmarks – Higham Tower, Nepinak Park and the Morgan War Memorial. If the stories about the McIntyre ghosts were true after all – if they were still in this house watching over Andersonville – they sure had a good view.

Nick's stomach growled. He had run out of the restaurant last night without eating, which meant that his last meal had been lunch yesterday. His stomach growled again, as if for emphasis. Food was one of those details that couldn't be ignored. He had to eat. Then he remembered that it had been hot dog day at school yesterday, but his mom had forgotten and made his lunch anyway, and it was still in his backpack.

Nick ran down the stairs two at a time. His backpack was right where he had left it. He snatched it up, raced back down the hall and, jump-kicking the front door shut, tore back up to the second floor. Suddenly he felt amazingly lighthearted, and he wanted to enjoy his lunch in the daylight. He ran through the upstairs rooms, searching for the perfect lunch spot. He tried two of the rooms, but the view wasn't quite right. He wanted to be able to look directly down on the stone stairs and Old Hill Road.

Finding the room he wanted, Nick took hold of the glass doorknob and turned it, but nothing happened. He jiggled it. Nothing. It must be stuck, he thought. He jiggled it again, leaning his shoulder into the door just in case it was jammed. It wasn't. It was locked.

That was strange. All the other rooms had been open – even the front door hadn't been locked! Perhaps it was being used for storage, Nick decided. There was no furniture in the rest of the house. Maybe everything of value had been locked up in one room.

Nick ate in one of the other rooms.

He liked this old house. It could use some paint and a good cleaning, but otherwise it was … friendly. If he hadn't been so upset over his problems, he might have been excited about this adventure. It would have been a great secret to share with his friends. But it wasn't that easy.

Nick thought about his mother. Did she wonder where he was? His heart told him she must be really worried. He'd never gone anywhere without telling her. But his head could only see Cole and the baby his mother was going to have. If they had replaced him, did she really care about him? The argument raged in Nick's head until finally he fell asleep again.

The storm broke in the late afternoon, bringing with it darkness. It was late in the year for an electrical storm, but it struck with a fury. The thunder grumbled and then boomed as great forks of white lightning ripped the sky, lighting it up more brightly than daylight. Then the rain came, lashing the old house with stinging pellets.

But Nick slept through the thunder and the lightning. He slept through the hammering of the rain on the windows. What woke him was the creaking of the front door hinges.

He hadn't shut the door properly, he figured – the wind had blown it open. But in darkness once again, the house didn't seem quite as friendly, and Nick wasn't willing to grope his way downstairs to shut the door. He listened hard. At first there was nothing, and then – his breathing stopped as he strained his ears. Yes! He heard it again.

It was a combination of a squish and a squeak. And then, as the sounds became louder, a bump was added. *Squish. Squeak. Bump. Squish. Squeak. Bump.* Whatever it was, it was coming up the stairs. Nick inched himself into a corner. What if the McIntyre ghosts were coming to get him? He imagined zombies with their flesh falling off in clumps. He pictured evil, grinning spirits he could see through. Nick knew he was a goner.

It had reached the top of the stairs. Now it was just *squish, squeak* again. But it was coming toward him – it knew where he was. Nick could barely hear the sound over the pounding of his heart. He squeezed his eyes shut. He couldn't bear to look. If he was going to die, he didn't want to know.

Then it stopped. Nick's eyes flew open. At that instant, a boom of thunder and a crack of lightning split the night.

And he saw it.

CHAPTER V

It WAS A GHOST — AND LIKE A CANDLE, IT WAS MELTING toward the floor.

Then the lightning was gone and the room was black again. Suddenly there was another explosion of light, this time directly in Nick's eyes, blinding him. Unlike the lightning, this light didn't go away.

"Why are you still here?" a voice demanded from the blackness beyond the light.

Nick gulped. He'd been right. The McIntyres had waited for him to leave and he'd blown his chance. He opened his mouth, but no sound came out.

"What do you want?" the voice asked impatiently.

"N-n-nothing," Nick stammered. "N-n-nothing. I-I don't want nothing."

"Anything," the voice snapped. "You don't want anything. Don't your parents teach you how to speak properly?"

Did ghosts correct people's grammar?

"You've run away, haven't you?" The voice chuckled evilly. "Well, aren't you the clever one?"

"W-what do you mean?" Nick asked, not sure he wanted to know. He held up his hand against the glare and wished the light biting his eyes would go away.

"Thought running away would solve all your problems, didn't you, boy?"

Nick was uneasy. He didn't like the direction the voice's questions were taking.

"Do you really think it's that easy? Do you?" The voice seemed angry and was becoming louder and more shrill. "Don't you know that when you run away from one set of problems, you only run toward a whole batch of new ones?"

Nick didn't know what to say. There was a horrible silence and then the voice whispered, so low and so slow it turned Nick's blood to ice, "Don't you know this house is haunted?"

The blinding light disappeared, and the horrible blackness was filled with a menacing, evil laugh that seemed to bounce off the walls in every direction. Nick covered his ears, but it didn't help. The ghost's head appeared above him, floating bodiless in the night.

Then, as quickly as it had appeared, the head vanished. There was a bump against the far wall and thumps and thuds as something – the ghost? –

settled to the floor. The laughing gradually subsided until it was nothing more than an amused echo.

Nick couldn't stand it any longer.

"Who are you?" he whispered.

"Who do you think I am?" the voice hissed back.

Something about it seemed familiar. "Do I know you?" Nick asked.

"Does anyone really ever know anyone else?"

Nick's fear was giving way to frustration.

"Do you always answer a question with a question?"

"What do you mean?"

"That!"

"What?"

"That! You just did it again. Every time I ask you something, you answer with a question."

"Do I?"

"You see! You see! You did it again."

"Are you trying to make me angry, boy?" the bodiless head appeared and disappeared again.

But it was long enough.

"I *do* know you!" Nick shouted into the darkness.

"Well, I admit we have run into each other." The head appeared again, and Nick realized it was a flashlight held under its chin that lent the head its eerie, bodiless appearance.

"You aren't a ghost at all."

"Well, not yet anyway, but I did enjoy the practice." Luther chuckled again. "In fact, that was the most fun

I've had in years."

Being the brunt of a huge joke made Nick indignant. "That was pretty cruel. You could've given me a heart attack or something."

"Somehow I doubt that. Kids your age don't often have heart attacks. They sometimes wet themselves, but they don't have heart attacks. And besides, you had it coming. Call it getting even."

"But I didn't mean to run into you!" Nick protested. "That was an accident. I told you I was sorry."

"So you did," Luther answered dryly. "Tell me, then, why didn't my scratches and bruises vanish the instant you apologized? And why didn't those miserable little twigs just fall from my hair? Hmm? Tell me."

"But you scared me on purpose!"

"And why shouldn't I? You're trespassing."

"But the McIntyres are all dead."

"True."

"So how could I be —" Then Nick understood. "*You* live here?" He was incredulous.

Luther nodded.

"Yes. Glamorous as life on a park bench might seem, there are times when a roof over one's head has definite advantages." There was a flash of lightning and then a rumble of thunder. A gust of wind threw a sheet of rain against the window. "Like tonight, for instance."

Luther still held the flashlight under his chin, and Nick realized why he'd thought his features were melting. Luther was drenched. He must have been caught in the storm.

"I didn't know," Nick said.

"You weren't supposed to. Nobody does. Let's keep it that way. I don't much like the idea of paying rent."

They were silent while they both thought about the situation. Then Luther said, "Well, since you're pretty much a boarder, you might as well tell me your name. I can't keep calling you *boy*."

"Nick Battle," Nick offered. When Luther didn't introduce himself in return, he asked, "Who are you?"

Luther seemed surprised. "Luther."

"Luther what?"

"How many other Luthers do you know?"

"None. But you have to have a last name."

Luther raised an eyebrow. "Oh, really? Why so?"

Nick scowled. "Huh? What the heck does that mean?"

"Why so?"

"Yeah, that."

"How come."

"Because I don't know what it means!" Nick's voice was loud with irritation.

Luther chuckled. "No, no. I wasn't asking you why you wanted to know. I was telling you what 'why so' means. It means 'how come.'"

Nick was embarrassed – and then annoyed again.

"Oh. Why didn't you say that in the first place? Now I forget what we were talking about."

Luther looked away and cleared his throat.

"My apologies," he said. "You were about to enlighten ... I mean, to explain why I must have a sur ... that is, a last name."

"Everybody's got a last name," Nick stated the obvious.

Luther seemed to be considering this. "I see. That's your argument, then? Because everyone else you know *has* a last name, I must have one too. Does that mean that if everyone else you know also has warts, I must have them as well?"

Nick looked hard at Luther. "You are really weird," he said. Then he threw up his hands. "Why can't you just tell me your name?"

"I told you – I don't have one."

Nick stuck out his chin belligerently. "I don't believe you."

Luther shrugged.

Nick tried again. "What's the big deal? You could make something up, and I wouldn't know the difference."

Luther pretended to be shocked. "Do you want me to lie?"

"That's not what I meant."

"Then you want me to be honest? Sincere?" Luther wasn't smiling, but Nick had the uncomfortable feeling he was making fun of him. When Nick didn't say anything, Luther carried on. "Then that's what I'll be – sincere. I shall be Luther Sincere."

It didn't seem that funny to Nick, but Luther laughed out loud. Then, just as quickly, he scowled at Nick and demanded, "Now, what in blazes are you doing in my house? Considering your late arrival last night and the fact that you're still here, I'd say you've run away. Right?"

"How'd you know I was here last night?"

"After you ran me over and then took off again like a scared rabbit, I watched you. When you headed up Old Hill Road, I knew you had to be coming here. The boards pried off the front door confirmed it. So I checked out the place, and there you were, sound asleep on the floor. I figured you'd get over whatever was bothering you and head for home today, no harm done." He paused. "But you're a stubborn little cuss. You're still here. I waited as long as I could, but that wind is mean, and the rain is cold."

"I can't go home," Nick said flatly.

"Why not?"

"They don't want me."

"Why? Are you one of those problem kids?"

"My mom's going to have a baby."

"Moms do that. That's how they get to be moms."

"You don't understand."

"You have that right. So, unless you have an urgent appointment this evening, why not explain it to me?"

So Nick did. He told Luther about growing up with just his mom, about Cole barging into his life. He explained how his mother was different now — and so was their home life. Then he told Luther about the baby.

"They didn't even ask me. They didn't care how I felt about having a baby around!" he wailed. "They just decided all by themselves. And why does my mom want a baby anyway? She's got a twelve-year-old kid. Why start having babies?"

"Haven't you ever wanted a brother or sister?" Luther asked.

Nick shrugged. "I never thought about it."

"So what are you going to do?"

"What do you mean?"

"Exactly what I said. What are you going to do? What are your plans? Where are you going to go? How are you going to eat? Where are you going to sleep? Winter's coming. What are you going to do for warm clothes? You have some decisions to make."

"Can't I stay here?" Nick blurted out. "Just for a while?"

"Ha!" Luther snorted. "Do I look like a man of wealth to you? I have enough trouble keeping myself alive without worrying about some runaway kid. If you don't want the home you have, fine. Leave it. That's your choice. But don't think you can push your way in here. I'm not looking for a roommate, and I'm sure as heck not looking to become a parent."

"But I won't be any trouble, I promise. I'll stay out of your —" The creaking of the front door hinges stopped Nick in mid-sentence. "What's that?" Luther's hand flew up over Nick's mouth.

"Shh," Luther whispered. "Don't move. Don't make a sound."

There were footsteps downstairs – more than one set. And there were voices, though they were too muffled to be understood. Then, one of the voices shouted, "Hello! Nick Battle, are you here?"

Nick nearly jumped out of his skin.

"It's the police, Nick! We've come to take you home! Your parents are worried about you," the officer shouted into the empty house.

How had the police found him? How had they known where to look? No one knew where he was – except Luther! It must have been Luther. He was the only one who knew Nick was here. He pushed Luther's hand away from his mouth.

"Why'd you tell them where I was?" he hissed.

"Are you crazy?" Luther whispered back. "Why would I lead the police here? If they find you, they find me. And I doubt they're bringing me a house-warming gift."

"C'mon, Gledhill," one of the officers said, "let's try the second floor. Maybe he's up there."

Nick didn't know what to do. He wasn't ready to go home, but if he didn't give himself up, they would find him anyway – and Luther too. And if Luther *hadn't* told the police, then …

He could see their flashlights on the hall wall. The police had nearly reached the top of the stairs.

"Nick Battle, are you up here?" the officer shouted again.

"Yes," Nick said quietly. He walked down the hallway toward the stairs, his backpack in his hand.

"Thank goodness." The officer was obviously relieved. "Are you all right? Your folks are worried sick. Let's get you home."

The other officer was talking into a small two-way radio. "We've got him. He's fine. Notify his family. We're on our way."

The officers escorted Nick down the stairs and out into the storm. As Nick reached the bottom of the stone steps, he looked back at the house, but it looked deserted.

CHAPTER VI

Nick's great adventure was the talk of the school for a week. Nick had run away. Not only that, he'd survived a whole night and a major electrical storm in a haunted house. Nick was a hero.

At first he felt embarrassed. He hadn't run away to impress anyone. He hadn't even planned it. Running away had just happened, and Nick was as surprised as anyone – and more confused.

Still, part of him was flattered by all the attention, and it didn't take him long to act the part. Nick told his friends what they wanted to hear. He said he'd wanted to find out if the McIntyre place really was haunted, and the only way to do that was to spend the night there. The terrifying details were all too clear, and Nick relived them when telling his stories.

He didn't actually lie, but he didn't tell his friends everything either. He didn't tell them the real reason he'd run away – that hurt too much to talk about. He also didn't tell them how alone and frightened he'd felt — that would make him look like a sissy. And he didn't tell them that the McIntyre ghost was actually a man named Luther. But that was partly to keep Luther's hideaway a secret.

"It was so-o-o dark that even a match couldn't have made a hole in the night. It wrapped itself around me so tightly I couldn't move. It was … unnatural," Nick whispered in a stilted voice.

"Weren't you scared?" someone whispered back.

Nick shrugged. "What choice did I have? Inside the house or out in the storm. A ghost or the lightning."

"Man, I would've picked the lightning," someone said, and everyone giggled nervously.

"Just a head, no body. It floated in a bubble of light right above me. And it was melting," Nick continued.

"What do you mean, *melting*?" someone interrupted. "Like a candle? You mean its hair and skin and everything were dripping off, just like melted wax?"

Nick nodded like one of the expressionless zombies he'd seen in the horror movies he wasn't supposed to watch.

"Ooh, that's gross!" someone squealed.

"It was hideous!" Nick hissed. "It had long scraggly hair, sunken eyes, and yellowish skin. And it was really angry. You could see it in its eyes. It didn't

41

want me there. It was laughing a horrible blood-chilling laugh. I didn't want to look at it, but I couldn't help myself. It was like it *made* me look."

"And then what?" they chorused anxiously.

"And then the police came stomping through the front door, and the head vanished."

Nick's story had the effect he wanted it to: his friends were sure to stay as far from the McIntyre mansion as possible.

After a week or so, the fuss died down, and things pretty much got back to normal. Nick's mother explained how they'd found him. The police had relayed a missing person report to all the buses, and the driver on the Kirkland Avenue route had remembered Nick right away. After that, it didn't take the police long to guess where Nick had gone. So Nick was glad he hadn't told anyone about Luther.

But the thought of Luther made Nick uncomfortable. Luther wasn't just an Andersonville curiosity anymore. He was a person, and Nick couldn't help wondering if he was getting enough to eat, and if his clothes would keep him warm through the winter. Why Nick cared, he wasn't sure. But he did. Whenever he was on Kirkland Avenue, he scanned the streets for a sign of the old vagrant, but he never saw him.

To his surprise, Nick hadn't been punished for running away. His mother had cried, and even Cole had seemed relieved to have him back. They'd been insensitive, they said. They should have realized that the idea of a new baby would upset him. They should have given him more time to adjust to their marriage.

By the time they were finished apologizing, Nick was convinced they were darn lucky to have him back. He might even have taken advantage of this if his mom hadn't been so sick. She kept throwing up, and always seemed to be tired. It was all part of having a baby, she said, but Nick wasn't so sure. Her skin was gray and she had dark circles under her eyes. The only time she didn't sleep was when she went to work, and she'd even called in sick a few times. Nick had always thought that pregnant women got fat, but his mother was losing weight.

Cole seemed worried too. He hovered like a nurse, plumping pillows, bringing tea and toast and giving neck massages. He took on all the housework – he vacuumed, did laundry and even cooked.

"Well, how's the chicken?" Cole asked one night when Nick and Cole were having supper alone for the third time in a row.

"Okay," Nick admitted grudgingly. The meal was really good, but Nick wasn't about to say so. "Where'd you learn to cook?"

"I was a bachelor before I married your mom. You can only live on Kraft Dinner for so long before you start looking like a piece of macaroni."

"Hey, I like Kraft Dinner," Nick protested.

"So did I until I'd eaten a thousand boxes of it. Once I was sick of that, I moved on to hot dogs, and after I'd learned to hate them, I overdosed on toasted tomato sandwiches. My mother finally gave me a cookbook. More chicken? There's lots left, what with your mom not eating."

"Thanks." Nick helped himself. "Is she really all right? She looks awful." As angry as he was with his mother for having a baby, Nick was still worried about her. And although Cole was responsible for the whole mess, he was the only one Nick could ask.

"She says she's fine." Cole smiled. "A woman goes through a lot of changes when she's expecting a baby. That's why she's so tired. But once her body gets used to its new job, your mom will be her old self again."

"When will that be?"

"I can't say for sure," Cole shrugged. "But the first few months are supposed to be the toughest. I bet your mom is just about through it by now."

"I sure hope so," Nick sighed.

Cole ruffled Nick's hair and, for some reason, Nick forgot to get mad.

"So do I," Cole confided with a wink. "I don't mind cooking, but I sure hate cleaning up."

That night, Nick had trouble getting to sleep. His thoughts kept chasing one another. He still wanted things back the way they used to be, but he was finding it harder and harder to dislike Cole, because Cole must really love his mom. She looked horrible, and she was no fun, but Cole kept fussing over her as if she was a princess. That had to be love. Besides, Cole wasn't mean to him. Nick almost wished he was – then it would be easy to hate him. But was Cole nice to him just because of his mom? Did Cole wish Nick wasn't there? And having a man in the house made Nick wonder about his father. Cole was really excited about becoming a father. Obviously Nick's father hadn't felt that way about him. It hurt to think about that.

Then there was the baby. Would his mom still love him as much once she had this baby? Nick wished he had someone to talk to, someone who would understand. Sure, he had friends, but his mom had always been the one he talked to about important things. But not anymore. Cole had ruined that.

Nick tried to push his problems out of his mind. His thoughts wandered to Luther instead. He hadn't told anyone about Luther. They wouldn't understand. His friends would see nothing more than a dirty vagrant. They would make fun of him and the way he lived on the streets. His mother would probably feel sorry for Luther, but he didn't need pity. He had pride. Nick was sure there was more to Luther than there seemed to be. He wished he could see Luther again. That would help him solve the mystery, he decided, as he finally drifted off to sleep.

The next day, Nick was up before the alarm. The morning was cold and crisp, and the weather office was forecasting the first snow of the season. Nick's class was going on a science field trip. An international inventors' convention was being held at the Capizzi Center, and they were going to see the exhibits. Nick was excited. He loved field trips – the bus ride, the singing, the laughing, just being out of school with all his friends – it was so much fun.

When the bus opened its door in front of Capizzi Center, Nick and the rest of his class spilled out as if from a corn popper. Nick was in the middle of a game of keep-away with a girl's glove.

"Throw it here," a boy yelled, backing up for the long pass.

Nick waved the glove in the girl's face, just out of her reach. When she lunged for it, he hurled it over her head toward the other boy. His pass was too long, and the boy had to back up and then jump. He caught it, but came down right on top of a litter container – and Luther.

"Gee, Mister, I'm really sor —" the boy scrambled to keep his balance – and Luther's, too – but when he saw who he had crashed into, his whole attitude changed. "Watch where you're going, old man!" he sneered. And then he brushed his clothes off as though Luther had dirtied him.

"Yeah, and take a bath!" one of the other boys yelled, holding his nose.

Through the laughter a girl said, "That's mean. He can't take a bath." Then she pointed to the garbage can. "He's too busy shopping."

There was more laughter and a flurry of insults and finger pointing before Nick's teacher took control.

"That's enough!" he barked. "Line up at the door. All of you." And then he turned to Luther. "I'm terribly sorry," he said. "Are you all right?" He grinned nervously. "You know how kids are – they don't really mean any harm, they just don't think."

Nick stood frozen, watching and listening. If he hadn't thrown the glove, none of this would have happened. He was angry – with himself and with his classmates. But if he didn't already know Luther, would he have joined in their teasing? He was ashamed of his friends and himself, and he was humiliated for Luther. Yet Luther hadn't said a word, or even given them a dirty look.

"Nick, stop gawking and get in line." His teacher was heading toward the entrance. If Luther recognized Nick, he never let on, didn't even look in his direction.

The day was spoiled for Nick. He had no interest in the exhibits and just wanted to be left alone to think. The Capizzi Center was so crowded that it was easy for Nick to slip away. At first he rambled aimlessly through the exhibition and then headed down the escalator to the lobby. It was very warm and stuffy, and he needed some fresh air. He looked out through the glass wall facing the escalator, and his spirits perked up a bit. It was snowing, quiet and soft and friendly. It seemed to brighten everything up.

Nick wanted to stand outside and lift his face to the first feathery dusting of winter. He knew it would help to push away his black mood. He ran the rest of the way down the escalator and through the foyer to the main entrance. But before he got to the doors, he stopped short.

There was Luther, standing just inside the entrance against a hot-air vent, his wire cart beside him. He was alternately blowing on his hands and rubbing his ears, trying to get warm. Nick started toward Luther, but a security guard cut in front of him.

"You know you can't stand here, Luther," the security guard said. He pointed to a sign above Luther's head. "You know the law. No loitering. I'm going to have to ask you to leave."

"Yeah, yeah," Luther nodded. "I know. Five minutes?" He held up his open hand hopefully. "Just five minutes. I'll stay out of the way. I just want to warm up a bit."

The guard looked uncomfortable.

"Look, Luther, I don't make the rules. I'm just

doing my job. It's nothing personal. It's the same for everybody."

"Is it?" Nick heard himself ask, and was surprised by his nerve.

Luther and the security guard both turned to look at him.

"Is it the same for everyone?" Nick demanded. "If Mayor Kaur stopped in to warm himself up, would you throw him out?"

The guard turned to Nick. He had an amused expression on his face. "And who might you be? The Lone Ranger?"

"Just answer my question." Then he added, "Please. Would you throw the mayor out?"

The man sobered. "Well, it's hardly the same thing."

"Why?" Nick argued. "Because the mayor is better dressed? Because the mayor has somewhere else to go?"

"Look, son," the security guard said quietly, "you're right. And I don't like it any better than you do, but there's nothing I can do about it. If I don't do my job, I'll lose it. And then I'll be looking for some place warm to stand, too."

"But it's wrong!" Nick was almost shouting.

The guard shrugged. "If you can change the system, more power to you. But I've got to do my job." Then he turned back to Luther. But the old vagrant was gone.

CHAPTER VII

Nick was totally frustrated. His life was one huge minefield, and he couldn't take a step without setting off a bomb.

Every time Nick showed up, Luther found trouble. He'd run Luther down on the street. He'd nearly had him kicked out of the McIntyre mansion. Because of him, Luther had been harassed by Nick's classmates and thrown out of the Capizzi Center. All Nick wanted to do was to help Luther, but everything kept going wrong. Just like his own life had gone wrong since Cole had arrived.

It occurred to him that Luther might feel about him the same way that he felt about Cole. No, that was stupid. They weren't alike at all. But the mere thought of Cole increased Nick's foul mood.

Nick slammed the door on his way into the house. His mother's startled face appeared around a corner.

"Hello? What's that all about?"

"Sorry," Nick mumbled. He felt guilty and defensive at the same time. "It slipped."

"So how was your day – or dare I ask?"

Nick shrugged without looking at his mother. "It was okay. I'm going to my room."

"Josh called just before you came in. He has your Walkman. Apparently you left it on the bus. Also, he would like his *Sports Illustrated* back if you're finished with it. You might want to give him a call."

"That's okay. I'll see him on Monday."

"Or we could drop it off tonight on our way to the game."

Nick groaned. He'd forgotten about the hockey game. Normally, he wouldn't miss a chance to see a game, but tonight he couldn't stand the thought of being with his mother and Cole for even five minutes.

"I'm not going," he said, and headed for his room.

"Excuse me?" His mother stopped him.

"I said I'm not going to the game."

"Just like that." She snapped her fingers. "May I ask why?"

"What's the big deal? It's just a game."

"I can't believe what I'm hearing. What's the big deal? I'll tell you what the big deal is, young man. Cole went to a great deal of trouble – not to mention expense – to get seats right behind the players' bench, Nick. To please you."

KRISTIN BUTCHER

"To buy me!" Nick glared.

His mother was stunned for a minute.

"Is that what you think? That Cole got those tickets to *buy* your affection? Tell me, when there was just you and me, Nick, and I took you places or gave you gifts, was I trying to buy you? We're a family, Nick. First there was you and me. Now there's Cole. And soon there will be the baby. Families don't *buy* each other, Nick. Think about that. And while you're at it, think about changing your clothes and finding Josh's magazine. We'll take it to his house on the way to the game."

Nick had taken his bad mood out on his mother. He'd expected her to be upset, but he hadn't expected her to snap at him. He'd better do what he was told.

The evening was a blur. He was so caught up in his own thoughts that he barely noticed his mother, Cole or the game. But by the next morning, Nick had made a decision. He was going back to the McIntyre place. His mother wouldn't like it, but she'd never actually forbidden him to go there again. Besides, he didn't intend to tell her. He wasn't sure, though, what sort of welcome Luther would give him. Never mind. He was going anyway.

Cole was at the paper. Nick's mother was having tea in bed and would probably stay there for a while, so it was the perfect opportunity.

Nick rummaged through the hall closet as quietly as he could. He found a hat, warm gloves and socks, and a winter parka that Cole no longer wore, but he still needed boots. If Luther had to wear his worn-out shoes all winter, he'd freeze for sure. Nick didn't dare take a pair of boots he knew Cole would look for, so he settled on some gum boots that no one would miss until spring. They wouldn't keep Luther's feet warm, but they would keep them dry, and with the heavy socks, they might not be too bad. Anyway, Nick figured, stuffing the boots into his sports bag, they had to be an improvement over Luther's shoes.

Nick was smiling to himself. At last he could help Luther.

Nick didn't recognize Old Hill Road. Now that the trees were bare, it was much brighter, and beneath its light blanket of snow, it was like an enchanted forest.

On top of its white mountain, the red-brick McIntyre mansion seemed to be frowning. But Nick was determined to deliver his gift, and nothing was going to put him off. He started toward the stone steps and then stopped. If Luther saw Nick coming and didn't want to talk to him, he could easily hide until Nick left. And if Luther was out, he would see

Nick's footprints in the snow when he returned and could stay out of sight until Nick went home.

Nick peered at the steps. Strange, he thought. There were no footprints. Hadn't Luther returned since yesterday's snowfall? His next thought panicked him – had Luther abandoned the McIntyre mansion? Had the authorities found him out? Nick wouldn't believe that. Luther was too clever.

Then Nick remembered his first visit to the McIntyre place. The front door had been boarded up, but Luther had lived there even then. That meant there had to be another way to get into the house. Nick fleetingly searched the bushes on each side of the stone path. At first he could see nothing, but then, beyond the bushes to his right, he thought he saw another pathway, just a trickle of a trail. And there were footprints in the snow.

The problem was how to get to it. There was no way through the bushes – they were thick and thorny.

Nick walked back down past the gate, scanning Old Hill Road for an entrance to the hidden pathway. About thirty feet past the gate, he found it, though if he hadn't been on the lookout, he never would have noticed it.

The trail wove its way through the woods, meandering around trees and bushes and gradually becoming more steep. The footprints continued, and Nick followed them until he found himself at the side of the house, in front of a simple, whitewashed, wooden door with a rusting doorknob – Luther's entrance.

The door's hinges creaked loudly. Inside, Nick was confronted with a narrow flight of stairs. At the top was yet another door leading to a tiny room lined with shelves. He slid open a door in one of the walls and passed through into the kitchen.

"Well done," Luther said from behind him.

Nick spun around.

"Did you have to do that?" he grumbled.

"Do what?" Luther smiled innocently.

"You know darn well what. Scare me! You seem to get a real thrill out of scaring me."

"Oh, come now. Don't sulk, Master Battle. You come looking for adventure and, when you find it, you whine. That's hardly the stuff of heroes. I'm surprised at you, especially after your gallant duel of words with the security guard at the Capizzi Center yesterday." There was an amused sparkle in Luther's eyes, and Nick was sure that Luther was making fun of him again.

"Where did you go?" Nick asked.

Luther shrugged. "Out. I hate to wear out my welcome." His voice became more stern. "Which doesn't appear to be a courtesy you worry too much about. You seem to be popping up on my doorstep quite regularly – uninvited, I might add."

Nick dropped the sports bag at Luther's feet.

"I brought you this," he said quietly.

Luther scowled at the bag.

"What is it?"

"Just some stuff."

"What sort of *stuff*?" Luther demanded.

Suddenly, Nick wasn't sure that his gift was such a good idea.

"Well?" Luther barked again.

"Just some stuff I thought you could use. Some winter clothes — a hat, some gloves, that sort of thing," he mumbled.

"Forget it." Luther didn't shout, but he was obviously angry. "Take your little donation right back where it came from. I don't need your charity!"

Now it was Nick's turn to be angry.

"Like heck you don't! Would you rather freeze to death? Or, or — no, wait, I know. You'd like it better if I chucked all this stuff in a garbage can somewhere, so you could get it yourself, right? That makes sense. Garbage is way better than charity!" Nick slapped his forehead with the heel of his hand. "Stupid me! What could I have been thinking?"

Luther was glaring hard at Nick, but Nick stared right back. Finally, Luther started to laugh. It was an amazingly full, deep laugh for such a small man.

"That's what I like about you, Nick Battle," he said. "You've got spunk. Not much sense," he added, "but a lot of spunk."

"Then you'll keep the clothes?" Nick asked hopefully.

"Hmmph," was Luther's only reply.

Nick stayed for about an hour. Luther was gruff and dodged Nick's questions, but Nick's worries were so near the surface that he did most of the talking. And Luther was a good listener. He didn't laugh at Nick's feelings. He didn't tell him that everything would work out. He didn't give him advice. He just listened. Every now and again he'd ask a question, but mostly he just let Nick ramble on. By the time he was ready to leave, Nick felt better — lighter somehow, as though he'd been carrying around a sack of rocks, and he'd finally been able to put it down. Nothing about his life had changed, but talking about it had helped.

"Can I come back sometime?" Nick asked as he was leaving.

"*May* I come back," Luther corrected him.

"*May* I come back?" Nick repeated. And then added, "Are you a teacher or something?"

"Why do you ask?"

"Because you're always correcting my grammar."

"Someone has to."

Nick shook his head in disgust.

"Now what's your problem?" Luther scowled.

"You. You never answer my questions."

"Perhaps you ask things that are none of your business."

Nick was thoughtful for a few seconds. Then his face cleared.

"Maybe," he shrugged. "Anyway, can I – I mean, *may* I come back sometime?"

"Would you stay away if I said no?" Luther asked.

Nick grinned impishly. "Probably not."

CHAPTER VIII

Nick started visiting Luther every Saturday morning, and the visits quickly became the high point of his week. By Friday afternoon he would get excited, plotting the next day's trek to the McIntyre mansion. Sometimes he would take doughnuts or cookies or hot chocolate to share with Luther, and always the morning paper, because Luther made a point of keeping up with the news. But after the incident with the winter clothes, Nick was careful not to take anything Luther might misinterpret as charity.

During their visits, Nick still did most of the talking, and Luther did most of the listening, so that after a month of Saturday visits, Nick knew no more about Luther than he ever had. He knew about Luther's pride and his sense of humor. He knew his mannerisms and his moods. But he still didn't know anything about his life – past or present.

Luther was a mystery. He slept in his clothes and lived out of garbage cans, but he was the most intelligent person Nick had ever met. There wasn't any subject Luther didn't know about; when Luther spoke, Nick was mesmerized, partly by his knowledge and partly by his voice. He was eloquent, obviously well-educated. So why did he live as a bum?

That was the hard part: Luther didn't fit Nick's idea of a vagrant. People only lived on the streets if they had no other choice, didn't they? But someone as smart as Luther must have had a choice. So why had he chosen poverty, hunger and public humiliation? What could Luther be hiding from that was worse than those things?

Nick was determined to find out, but he was just going to have to wait until Luther decided to tell him. He would have to be patient.

In the meantime, he loved his Saturday morning visits and did as much as Luther would allow to make the old man's life easier. It seemed as if Luther had nothing. Things that Nick took for granted – a home, food, clothing, even a bathroom! – Luther did without. And he wasn't the only one. Nick wondered why he'd never really noticed street people before. There were so many of them. But until now – until Luther – they'd never touched Nick's life. He'd seen them hustling change at bus stops, picking cigarette butts up off the sidewalk, and checking pay phones for forgotten quarters, but all he'd ever felt was creepy. He'd never actually thought about these people. Now he couldn't get them out of his mind.

So when his teacher assigned a research project on life in Andersonville, Nick knew immediately what he'd do: a report on the life of street people. He already knew a lot because of Luther, but he needed more. Forgetting his resolution to keep his mother and Cole at a distance, Nick chattered enthusiastically at the dinner table about the assignment.

"That's a good angle," Cole complimented him. "I bet no one else will think to write about street people. Most people prefer to pretend they don't exist. The subject makes them uncomfortable."

"Exactly!" Nick agreed. "But, see, that's what I want to do. I want to make people uncomfortable. I want them to stop pretending that street people aren't there. I want them to do something to help."

Nick's mother and Cole exchanged glances.

"You seem to feel pretty strongly about this," his mother said. "How come?"

Nick shrugged.

"Um, well, I've been noticing street people a lot lately, and it's not right. People aren't supposed to live like that. We should be doing something to help."

"My son, the champion of causes," his mother smiled.

"Are you making fun of me?" Nick was suddenly defensive.

"No, no! Absolutely not," his mother replied quickly.

"Listen, Nick," Cole cut in, "I think what you're doing is super. And you're completely right. People do need to become aware. I just wish I'd thought of this. It would make a great human-interest series for the paper, especially with Christmas coming up. So, tell me, how are you planning to go about your research?"

Nick was flattered and, for the first time in a long time, he felt almost happy. He told Cole some of his ideas, and Cole gave him a few suggestions and the names of some people who might be able to give him information.

The assignment wasn't due until after the Christmas break but, for once, Nick didn't leave it to the last minute. He followed up the leads Cole had given him and collected more material than he could ever use. But he wasn't satisfied. He wanted his report to show that those who were forced to live on the streets were real people, not just statistics; he needed to interview some street people.

"No, Nick," his mother said. "I'm sorry. I can't allow you to do that."

"Why not? Nothing's going to happen. You said yourself that they're people just like us, only less fortunate. You said they only needed some help to turn their lives around. Was that just talk?"

"No, Nick. I meant what I said. Really." His mother was obviously uncomfortable. "But these people have to do anything they can just to stay alive. Desperate people can do desperate things. Nick, you're only twelve years old. You have no idea what to expect."

Nick held up his stack of research notes.

His mother frowned. "That's not the same thing. I don't care how much research you do. It can't possibly prepare you for the real thing. It's dangerous out there."

Nick started to say something, but his mother cut him off. "No. Just listen. If I let you do this thing, do you realize who you'd be dealing with? Drunks. Drug addicts. Dope dealers – and worse. I'm not saying it's their fault they ended up on the streets, but that's where they are. If they saw an unsuspecting kid like you walking around alone, they'd mug you just for your jacket."

"You're exaggerating," Nick protested. "They're not all drug addicts or drunks. There are many —"

"— thieves, murderers, perverts and child molesters," his mother interrupted. "Shall I go on?"

"Carol, take it easy," Cole said. "You're getting all worked up."

"You bet I am! And why shouldn't I?" she snapped. "What do you expect me to do – book him a mattress at a shelter?"

There was an uncomfortable silence. Finally, Nick broke it.

"Mom, I know there are horrible people on the street. But they're everywhere else too – parks, theaters, supermarkets, schools. They could be our neighbors and we don't even know it. According to my research —"

His mother sighed heavily and shook her head.

"Just listen?" Nick pleaded. "Would it hurt just to listen?"

His mother sighed again. "No," she conceded, "it wouldn't hurt. I'll listen, but I'm not going to change my mind."

Nick wanted to yell, but he forced himself to stay calm.

"According to my research, the streets are the only place the poor can go. The poor, Mom. More than anybody else, that's who's out there. And being poor doesn't mean they're into drugs or crime. It means they can't find work. It means they're sick. It means they have no one to take care of them. It means they're hungry. The streets are all they have.

"When I started this report I wondered how people ended up on the street. I thought they were probably just too lazy to work. But that can't be right, because the people on the streets have to work all the time just to stay alive. You know where they live? In bug-infested apartments, maybe – if they're lucky enough to be on welfare. In abandoned cars, tents, cardboard boxes that fridges come in. The rest have to settle for even less – a bus shelter or a piece of sidewalk near a heating vent.

"Do you want to know the really scary part? There are more and more street people – and poor people – all the time. They're everywhere. I mean, just look at our neighborhood. Everybody's doing fine, right? So how come my school has a breakfast and lunch program to make sure students get some decent food? And how come Mr. Pacula down the street found a vagrant sleeping in his garage? This isn't going to go away. We have to face it and find answers. If my report is going to do any good, it has to be based on more than statistics. It has to be about real people. So I have to talk to those people. Don't you understand?"

Nick couldn't read his mother's expression, but her words were clear.

"I understand what you're saying, Nick, and you're right – something needs to be done. But you haven't convinced me that you'd be safe, and I will not have you putting yourself in danger for the sake of a school report. I'm sorry."

Nick had done his best. He hadn't lost his temper, screamed, cried or thrown anything. But he wished he had.

"That's not fair!" he wailed.

"Nick, your mother's right," Cole said.

Nick was instantly angry.

"Oh, yeah, sure! I should have known. I should have known!" he yelled. "For a little while there I thought you meant what you said about this being important! I should have known —"

"Now just hang on a minute," Cole cut short Nick's explosion. "Your mom is worried about what could happen to you. And she has every right to be concerned. What you're suggesting could be dangerous. But caring about your safety doesn't mean we don't want to help. Maybe we can compromise."

"Compromise?" Nick asked warily.

"Well … if it's okay with your mom," Cole glanced tentatively at his wife, "and with you, of course," he added hastily, "I could come with you when you do your interviews. I wouldn't interfere – I'd just make sure you're safe, okay? That way you could complete your research and your mom wouldn't have to worry. What do you say?"

Nick's instinct was to refuse Cole's offer, and his mind raced to find a reason to object. But before he could come up with anything, his mother had answered for him.

"Come on, Cole, you're no more experienced with street people than Nick is. I mean, this is not exactly the best part of town that we're talking about. I know you're trying to help, but I think I know what's best."

"Whoa! Hold it right there," Cole objected. "I may not have firsthand experience with this particular subject, but I *am* a journalist, Carol, and I *have* been in dangerous situations many times before. *And* I am very capable of taking care of myself, thank you. Besides, yes, you have to anticipate possible problems, but I don't think it's healthy to assume the worst is going to happen."

"I don't like it," she insisted.

"But you said that what I was doing was important!" Nick forgot about his own objections to Cole's suggestion to accompany him.

"It *is* important, Nick," his mother admitted grudgingly.

"Then why won't you let me do it? If I don't talk to these people, I can't learn anything that might help, and that's the whole point of this project. Okay, I'll compromise – not that anything *would* happen – but I'll go with Cole. Okay? If you don't let Cole come with me, that means you never meant anything you said about giving the poor a chance to turn their lives around." Nick's argument was convincing and he knew it, though he couldn't believe that he and Cole were actually on the same side.

He waited anxiously for his mother's decision. Finally, she let out a huge sigh of defeat.

"I don't know which one of you frustrates me more, but I'm obviously outnumbered. I still don't like it ... but I won't stop you."

CHAPTER IX

Nick and Cole set aside the following Sunday for the interviews. Nick would have liked to have made at least two trips — one during the day and one at night — but his mother had made it very clear that wandering around after dark was out of the question.

Nick prepared carefully. He made up pages of questions and made sure he had plenty of paper and sharp pencils. He checked his tape recorder and put in new batteries. Then he stocked up on film for his camera.

Nick and Cole decided to start at the Beacon Mission, Andersonville's shelter for the homeless. They parked the car there and interviewed the mission's employees. Then they worked their way on foot toward Pepper Park along Shore Street, an area Nick had seldom been through in a car, let alone on foot.

Everything was faded and lifeless, as though a dingy film had settled over the torn awnings, rusting lamp posts, street signs and people. Even the lightly falling snow seemed gray.

Nick and Cole barely spoke. Just by walking down the sidewalk, they had fallen under the spell of Shore Street. It was a commercial area – at least, it had been at one time. Now many of the buildings were abandoned. Some had even been torn down. But quite a few still housed businesses – grocery stores, drug stores, appliance dealers, second-hand shops – though, being Sunday, they were pretty quiet. Here and there, cowering between the commercial buildings, were tiny houses – old and run-down, but obviously occupied. Nick saw a tricycle on the porch of one house, heard music blaring from the depths of another, and glimpsed two small children staring at him from the window of a third. He noticed a bent basketball rim riveted to the wall of a warehouse and a hopscotch drawn on the sidewalk. People lived here.

He felt a jab in his side, and he jumped. Cole nodded toward a woman huddled in the doorway of a closed bookstore. She was tiny, so the once-purple coat with a rope tied around her middle nearly reached her ankles. It was stiff with grime and ripped at the shoulder, the collar pulled up against the cold. A heavy, ratty-looking hat nearly hid the woman's face, but at least it looked warm. Her gloves were fingerless. She was devouring the remains of a muffin, but her eyes darted about as if she expected her lunch to be snatched from her.

"There you go, Nick. There's someone to talk to."

Nick looked at Cole and then at the woman, who was now eying them warily. He took a deep breath. This was what he'd come for. Cole gave him a reassuring smile, and Nick started toward the woman.

Before he had taken two steps, she burst out of the doorway and fled down Shore Street.

"You keep away from me!" she screeched over her shoulder. "You keep away from me, you hear. I ain't done nothin'. Julianna ain't no thief. I ain't stole nothin'. This food's mine. I ain't took it."

"Please," Nick called after her, "I know you're not a thief. I just want to talk to you. Please!" But the woman was already half a block away and showed no signs of slowing down. She continued muttering as she shook her scrawny fist at Nick.

Helpless, Nick turned back to Cole.

"I wasn't going to hurt her. Why did she run away?"

Cole sighed. "I know you wouldn't hurt her, Nick. But she didn't know that. She was just protecting herself. Put yourself in her place – two males against one small woman. If we had been after her, she wouldn't have stood a chance."

Nick had to think about that for a minute, but he knew that Cole was right.

"So, now what? If I can't get anyone to talk to me, how am I going to find out about them?"

"Oh, I don't know," Cole said, as he resumed walking. "Didn't you get information from that woman?"

Nick had to think about that too. Then he had to run to catch up to Cole.

Nick wasn't naive enough to think that people were going to line up to be interviewed, but he had thought there would be more of them around. And the people they did see vanished by the time Nick and Cole got close.

"This is harder than I thought," Nick finally admitted, flopping down on a bench. "As soon as anyone sees us, they take off."

Cole sat down beside him.

"Well, nobody said journalism was easy. It's kind of like being a door-to-door sales rep. You keep getting doors slammed in your face, but you don't give up. That really big sale could be right behind the next door."

"Yeah, but I'm not even getting slammed doors. All I'm getting is nobody at home."

Cole chuckled. "Well, sometimes you just have to bide your time until somebody comes home. You make use of that time in other ways."

Nick stopped fiddling with the camera in his lap and glanced up at Cole. Then he let his eyes travel the length of Shore Street.

"Maybe now would be a good time to take some pictures." It was more a question than a statement. "I can use those in my report too."

"Good idea," Cole nodded. "Just don't go too far. Stay where I can see you. I'll be right here."

So Nick wandered off, unsure at first of where to go or what to photograph. He snapped pictures of the street and of storefronts, trying to stuff as much as he could into each photograph without straying too far from Cole. But soon he became bolder, venturing into the mouths of alleys and investigating every nook and cranny he came across. He even peered into the window of a house he'd thought was deserted, only to discover a big, balding man in an undershirt shaking his fist at him. That sent him scurrying for the safety of the sidewalk. The more he looked, the more he saw, and the more stories his photographs told. He snapped pictures of a man and woman carrying groceries, someone else walking a dog, and a shopkeeper sweeping the sidewalk in front of his store.

He became so caught up in his explorations that he forgot about Cole; he was a good block away and on the opposite side of the street before he thought to look back. Cole was still there on the bench, writing something in the small spiral notebook he always carried with him. But for some reason – perhaps he felt Nick's eyes on him – he looked up and waved. Nick waved back. Then Cole bent over his notebook once more, and Nick resumed his investigation of Shore Street.

He had reached the end of the block. He should probably head back, he thought. He glanced at Cole, who was still scribbling intently, and then he looked down Shore Street. It was empty.

Nick allowed himself a discouraged sigh. He wasn't getting anywhere. What good were a few pictures? He still needed to talk to the people. But what was he supposed to do? He couldn't make them appear out of thin air. He aimed his camera at the street sign, a cross of white metal strips, bent and rusting at the edges. Faded black lettering proclaimed the cross-roads – Shore Street and Hope Avenue.

Nick lowered his camera without taking the shot. Perhaps it was an omen. Perhaps Hope Avenue was where Nick would find his answers. He took one last look back at Cole. He wouldn't like it, but … then Nick slid around the corner.

If possible, Hope Avenue was even more depressing than Shore Street. There was no hope there, unless it was that the entire street might be bulldozed. It was barely wide enough for two cars. Probably not a problem, Nick realized, for there wasn't a car in sight. The buildings were mostly two-story, dressed up in gaudy reds and pinks and blues that had long ago grown tired. Heavy with years of accumulated dirt, the buildings sagged and leaned against each other to keep from toppling over. Their windows had been painted black, boarded over or smashed. Where the walls joined the street, the wind had planted cardboard coffee cups, yellowed newspapers, sodden cigarette packages and crumpled drink cans.

It was a horrible place. Worse than horrible. Nick shivered and his skin began to crawl. He didn't want to touch anything. He didn't even want to breathe the air. There were no answers on Hope Avenue.

As he turned to leave, a movement near the curb caught Nick's eye. At first, all he saw was an ancient fire hydrant, but then a man, equally ancient, rolled out from behind it and dragged himself to his feet. Even in his bulky gray cardigan the man was sickly thin, and his skin looked vacuum-packed to his bones in tight, wrinkled waves. Liver spots like huge freckles dotted his hands and balding head. He wore no gloves, no hat, yet seemed oblivious to the cold.

He was walking away from Nick, by the curb, and his steps were slow. Periodically he would stop, bend and make a slashing motion with his arm. Then he'd move on.

Nick couldn't let this chance slip away. He couldn't risk scaring this old man as he had Julianna. If these people didn't trust him because he was different, then he wouldn't *be* different. Stuffing his camera into his pocket, he ripped off his parka, hat and gloves, and crammed them into the narrow gap between two buildings. He looked down at his clothes – old jeans and a sweatshirt that had spent a few days in a heap on his bedroom floor. He scraped his fingers through a layer of sludge on a window sill and worked the oily grunge into his hands. Then he ran his hands through his hair and across his forehead. Finally, he wiped his hands on his sweatshirt. He wasn't sure if this would help him to fit in, but it couldn't hurt.

As Nick got close to the old man, he could hear him muttering, and strained to catch his words. Then, without warning, the man turned on Nick, as though he'd known he had been there all along.

"Is this your vehicle, sir?" the old man demanded in a raspy croak. The electricity in the man's watery-blue eyes bored into Nick. He hadn't been prepared for such energy. He also didn't understand the question.

"Are you deaf?" the man persisted. "I asked you a question. You see that chalk mark on your tire?" He pointed to an invisible line on the invisible tire of an invisible car. "I put that there over an hour ago." He shook his head and scowled. Then he pointed up to his right. "Can't you read? It says one hour parking from 9 A.M. to 5 P.M. You're in violation, sir."

Nick looked up, but there was no sign. No tire, no car, no sign. And he obviously wasn't old enough to drive. But he knew none of that mattered to the indignant, wizened old man.

"So, you have nothing to say for yourself, eh?" The old man harrumphed. "I'm not surprised. I've got you dead to rights. I'm going to have to write you up." He shook his imaginary pen under Nick's nose. "Maybe a fifty dollar fine will help you to read parking signs in the future. Name?" he barked.

Nick was startled. He didn't know what to do. The old man seemed harmless enough. Maybe Nick should go along with him, but the idea of taking part in this charade made him feel foolish.

"Look, I don't know —" he began, but the old man cut him off with a piercing glare.

"Save your excuses for court. All I'm interested in is filling out the particulars on this ticket." He fixed Nick with a scornful stare and, when Nick made no response, his blue eyes narrowed impatiently. "Fine. Don't tell me your name. I don't really need it. They'll trace it through your license plate."

"Nick Battle," Nick blurted. As crazy as the man seemed to be, Nick wanted to keep him talking.

The man seemed mildly surprised.

"Well," he rasped, "finally a little cooperation." He recorded Nick's name in his imaginary book and then pressed on. "Address?"

This time Nick answered without hesitation and watched in awe as his address was painstakingly recorded. So diligent was the old man about his task that Nick was almost convinced he could see the writing.

"License plate number?"

Nick found himself starting to enjoy the game. He volunteered Cole's plate number. "852 EXH."

The old man shuffled backward and leaned toward the curb. He wavered there a few seconds before urging his body back to its upright position. Then, before Nick realized what was happening, the man turned on him ferociously.

Nick gasped and backed away, but the old man's head was in his face and a tobacco-stained finger was hammering on his chest.

"What are you playing at?" the man wheezed. He was so close that Nick could see the milky cataracts glazing his eyes and a blue vein pulsing at his temple. The man's breath was sour and hot, and Nick's nostrils clenched against it.

"That's not your plate number!" The man was still poking Nick. "It's probably not even your real name. You stole that car, didn't you? Didn't you!"

Nick had backed himself right up against a building, and the old man's body was pressed tightly against his, trapping him. He couldn't free his arms. He couldn't breathe. He was terrified. Why had he left

Shore Street? Why hadn't he stayed where Cole could see him? Nick felt as though he was suffocating.

The old man was still ranting. Nick could see his lips moving, but the creak of his ancient voice was drowned out by a hot roaring, like a desert wind, in Nick's ears. It was getting louder and louder. Why couldn't he breathe? He had to get some air.

And then, suddenly, Nick was free. One second he was suffocating, and the next he had burst free. He couldn't remember pushing the old man away, but he must have. Instantly, cold air began pouring down on him, and he gulped it hungrily into his lungs. He fumbled along the wall, away from the old man, who had started shuffling toward him once more.

He turned to run, but his boot caught on something. Nick put his arms out to break his fall. The next thing he knew, he was hurtling into a dark passage toward a metal door.

He braced himself for the impact.

CHAPTER X

T HE DOOR WAS SLIGHTLY AJAR AND, WHEN NICK slammed into it, it flew open, leaving him sprawled across the doorsill.

He glanced back toward the street. There was no sign of the old man. Relief washed over him. It was crazy. Ten minutes ago, he'd been praying for a chance to get close to the old man. Now all he wanted was to stay as far away from him as possible. The man was old and frail, but he was also scary. His body was here on Hope Avenue, but his mind was somewhere else, and he had tried to force Nick to go there with him.

He shuddered at the memory and looked toward the street once more. He still couldn't see the old man, but he could hear him. Nick scrambled to his feet and ducked inside the building, out of the doorway. With any luck, the man would give up when he didn't see him.

Nick waited a minute, then cautiously peered out.

The old man was standing at the entrance to the passage, blinking blindly into the darkness. Nick pulled back quickly.

Darn! Now what was he going to do? He couldn't run back to the street without pushing the old man aside, and Nick was afraid of hurting him. There was still a chance the old man would just go away, so Nick decided to wait.

He turned away from the door. Bare electric bulbs dimly lit the hallway ahead. Nick squinted at the dark walls and the crumbling checkerboard floor. Did people actually live here? He became aware of a musty odor. But there was another smell mixed with it too, and it was coming from the end of the hall, from a door with a sign on it.

Forgetting the old man, he tiptoed forward until he was close enough to make out the words on the sign – *House of Hope, Free Food, All Welcome.* It was a soup kitchen, Nick realized, but before he could decide whether to go in, the door swung open. He jumped back. The mingled aromas of cooking food spilled into the hallway, along with the clatter of dishes and a plump middle-aged woman. She was buttoning her coat over a soiled white uniform. When she saw Nick, she grinned, displaying a mouthful of crooked, yellow teeth.

"You're just in time," she said. "The stew's fresh and hot and *de*-licious." She smacked her lips and rubbed her ample stomach. "Even if I do say so myself. You go in there and get yourself a bowl before it's all gone."

Nick blinked stupidly.

"Well, what are you waiting for?" the woman urged. "In you go."

"No, thank you." Nick started to back away. "That's all right. I'm not hungry. Really. I just …"

"Fiddlesticks!" The woman waved away Nick's protests. "Boys are always hungry." Then she paused and said kindly, "You're new. Are you on your own?" When Nick didn't answer, she patted his shoulder. "Never mind. You'll be all right. You're safe here. My name's Crystal."

She must have thought he was a runaway, Nick realized. "But I …" he began, but Crystal shushed him and hurried him through the door.

"Sit here," she said, steering him toward a trestle table along one wall. She pushed him down onto the bench behind the table. "Just sit here while I get you some stew." She shook a finger at him. "And don't move. I'll be right back."

Nick couldn't have moved if he'd tried. He was too stunned, or too afraid – he wasn't sure which. He felt as though pieces of himself kept falling off every time he took a step, every time he touched anything. All he'd wanted was to talk to people, not get caught in their world.

He looked around him. There were about a dozen people scattered about the room. A few men sat together, smoking and talking. There was a woman with an infant in a corner. A family took up a table in the center of the room. The rest sat alone, mechanically eating, staring blankly at their plates. Leftover people, Nick thought sadly.

As if reading his mind, someone looked up at him, and he self-consciously lowered his eyes to the plastic table cloth. It was scarred with cigarette burns and the circular impressions of countless coffee cups. Nick barely noticed. He was asking himself the question he'd asked so many times before. *How did people live like this?* Then an even more discomforting thought struck him. *How did people get like this?*

"Here you go," Crystal chirped, plunking a bowl down in front of Nick. Some of its contents spilled over the rim. "You'll feel better once you get some warm stew inside you. And I've brought someone to keep you company while you eat. This is Mac. He helps out around here, but right now he's on his break."

Nick looked up. A boy, about sixteen, looked back. He was dressed all in black – runners, sweatpants, sweatshirt, even the ball cap crammed backward over his slicked-back hair. His forehead was an acne war zone. His upper lip bore the fuzzy beginnings of a mustache. He stood slouched, cool, but his eyes were wary.

"Well, I gotta run," Crystal trilled. She waggled her fingers in a friendly farewell and hurried toward the door. Nick suddenly felt abandoned. It was silly – he didn't even know the woman – but still …

He looked down at the steaming bowl. It was more like lumpy water than stew. Bits of carrot, onion and potato floated in a liquid the color of dirty dishwater. Small pools of fat had formed on the surface, and Nick watched as they collided to form larger pools.

"I'm not really hungry," he said.

"Suit yourself." Mac shrugged, pulled the bowl toward him and slid onto the bench across from Nick. "I didn't like this stuff either when I first —" he hesitated, "came here. But it kinda grows on you." He slurped the stew noisily and then remarked, "You musta been in some hurry if you didn't even bother to grab a jacket."

Nick was startled. "What?"

Mac shook his head and snickered. "Man, you are really out of it. Winter? Snow? Cold? Coat? Remember? Or is your brain already frozen? Take it from me, kid, if you plan to make it on your own, you're going to have to wake up."

"Are *you* on your own?"

"A couple of years now. More or less. I sort of lose track." He gestured toward the kitchen area with his spoon. "But if it's macaroni and cheese, it's gotta be Monday. Chicken soup is Thursday." He laughed. "Besides, who cares? It's not like I got a dentist appointment or a math assignment due, know what I mean?"

Nick didn't really know, but he nodded anyway. "So, do you work here?" he asked.

"You mean, do I get paid?" Mac shook his head. "Nah. But the way I look at it, it's experience. You know, somethin' I can put on one of those résumé things. Hey, who knows, someday I just might be head honcho at one of those swanky restaurants with fancy table cloths and shiny silver." He sighed contentedly and pushed the bowl away. "I can see it now – me, with a snobby little black mustache, wearing a tuxedo, palming fifty dollar bills to seat rich dudes by the window or the fireplace." He chuckled again. "Cool."

"So where's your family?" Nick tried to sound casual, but Mac wasn't fooled.

"Who cares?" he snapped. He studied Nick through hooded eyes. "For a kid who's just run away, you're pretty nosy."

"Sorry," Nick apologized. So far, Mac was the only sane person he'd had a chance to talk to, and he didn't want to blow it. He tried to look upset. "I guess I was just thinking about myself."

Mac seemed to relax. He pointed a finger at Nick. "You'll get over it. Trust me."

"But don't you miss them?" Nick asked.

"Hey, sure, I miss them," Mac scoffed. "Their nagging, their yelling, trying to run my life!"

Nick looked away, but said nothing.

Mac continued more quietly. "Besides, they were happy when I left. So was I."

Nick couldn't believe that, and he wasn't convinced Mac believed it either.

"Didn't they look for you?"

"No way, man. It was their big chance and they took it. Packed up everything and moved. A couple of months after I left, I went back – just to see what was happening, right? There's this miniature park across from the house I used to live in. So I sat there one afternoon and watched." He shifted uneasily on the bench. "Okay, it was a stupid idea. I just wanted to see what they were doing, I guess, eh? Like I said, stupid. Got any cigarettes?"

Nick shook his head. Mac dug a handful of butts and a book of matches from the pouch of his sweatshirt and dumped them on the table.

"Take one."

Nick shook his head again. "No, thanks."

"Fine. If you change your mind, help yourself." Then he selected the longest butt, lit it and inhaled deeply. "Anyway, they weren't there. I waited around most of the afternoon. About five o'clock, this car drives up. I figured, hey, the old man got some new wheels. But, no. The guy who got outta the car was a total stranger. Goes right up to the front door, unlocks it, and walks in. I think I'm seeing things. Uh-uh. Not five minutes later, another car pulls into the driveway, this lady and two little kids. When they just walk into the house too, I know they gotta live there." Mac took another drag on his cigarette, squinting to keep the smoke out of his eyes.

Nick tried to comprehend what Mac had told him.

"So where did your parents go?" he asked finally.

"Who knows? Who cares?"

"Don't you?"

Mac looked hard at Nick. Then he said, "Listen, man. Either get over it or go home. Otherwise, you ain't gonna make it."

Just then, the crazy old man from the street shuffled through the door. Nick's uneasiness must have shown on his face, because Mac turned to look.

"Yo, Captain." He waved a greeting.

Without a glance in Mac's direction, the old man raised an arm listlessly in acknowledgment.

"You know him?" Nick asked.

"Yeah, sure." Mac turned back to Nick. "Everybody calls him Captain. He was in the army or navy or something – 'til they retired him. Then he worked for the city as one of those guys who gives out parking tickets. Eventually they retired him from that, too. After his wife died, Captain kinda slipped over the edge. He's gotta be ninety years old, but he's still handing out those parking tickets."

Nick followed Captain with his eyes and then looked around the room again. "Are all these people homeless?"

Mac hooted. "No way. A lot of 'em even have jobs. They don't make enough to live on, but they got jobs. The House of Hope just kinda helps 'em over the rough spots." He leaned across the table and grabbed Nick's arm. "Take my advice, kid," he said. "Get out of here. Go home while they'll still take you back." Then he pushed himself away from the table and walked away. But he called over his shoulder, "And hey, if you run away again, take a coat."

Before Nick had a chance to answer, he heard someone calling his name. He turned toward the voice and saw Cole standing in the entrance. Except for his lips, which were blue, Cole's face was white. He'd lost his hat somewhere, too, and his hair had fallen into his eyes. He was puffing as though he'd been running. And he was carrying Nick's parka, camera, gloves and hat. Nick shrivelled with guilt. He'd completely forgotten about Cole.

Cole strode toward Nick and threw the clothes on the table. For several seconds he just stood there, staring at Nick and panting. Finally, he said, "I thought I told you to stay where I could see you." He seemed to be fighting for control. "Do you have any idea what could have happened to you?"

Nick couldn't decipher the tone of Cole's voice. Was it anger, worry or relief? "I'm sorry," he mumbled. Then, when Cole just kept staring at him, he said it again. "Really. I really am sorry."

Cole opened his mouth to speak several times. Finally he said, "Damn it, Nick! You scared me to death!"

Nick could tell he meant it.

"Cole, I —"

"Let's get out of here," Cole said gruffly. As they made their way to the door, he put an arm around Nick's shoulder.

Nick looked up remorsefully. "Cole, I really am sorry."

"I know you are. Let's just thank our lucky stars that nothing happened. But if you ever do anything like that again, so help me, I'll personally skin you alive." Then he tweaked Nick's ear. "Do you hear me?"

Nick rubbed his ear. "I hear ya," he grimaced.

"Good. So, what did you find out?"

CHAPTER XI

WINTER HAD INCHED ITS WAY INTO ANDERSONVILLE
gently. There had been several soft snowfalls, but it
had remained mild. The sudden cold snap two weeks
before Christmas caught everyone off guard. Minus
thirty degree days caused people to abandon the
skating ponds and ski slopes for indoor activities.

Nick wasn't alarmed when he arrived at the
McIntyre mansion on Saturday morning to discover
Luther wasn't there. He had told Nick that he went
to the Beacon Mission when nights became too cold
to spend in the house. Nick knew that the shelter was
the town's only refuge for the homeless, and
sometimes there just wasn't enough room for them
all. Nick wondered if the people he'd met on Hope
Avenue would be there. Captain? Mac? Crystal?

Nick checked his watch. It was just after ten —
Luther would probably be along soon. Nick decided
to wait upstairs.

He liked the second floor because it let the light in and because he could see out from there. Also, the locked room fascinated him. He had asked Luther about it once, but as always, Luther had cleverly sidestepped the question. Nick no longer believed the room contained McIntyre valuables – he was sure it contained Luther's valuables. In the entire house there was no sign that Luther lived there – not a paper, not a blanket, not a scarf, nothing. Yet Nick knew Luther didn't pull his whole world around with him in his wire cart. He was forever collecting things. He had to put them somewhere, and Nick's guess was that they were in the locked room.

Nick knew the door would be locked, but out of habit, he tried the doorknob anyway. It turned. Nick's first thought was that Luther must be on the other side of the door, still asleep.

He pushed the door open cautiously and peeked in. No one was there – Luther had simply forgotten to lock the door. Nick knew he should shut the door and walk away. He knew how carefully Luther guarded his privacy. He was abusing Luther's trust, and if Luther ever found out, their friendship would be finished. Yet he couldn't walk away.

Something stronger than a sense of right and wrong kept Nick standing in the doorway. Something more powerful than his fear of the consequences pushed him into the room. It was more than curiosity.

Nick knew that Luther's identity had to be in this room, and that a horrible secret was destroying the man Luther had once been. If Nick could discover that secret, perhaps he could help Luther get his life back.

The room was discouragingly empty, and Nick was saddened to find that Luther's entire life could fit so easily into such a small space. To one side of the room, but away from the wall, were newspapers, stacked tightly to form a rectangular base about two feet high. On top of the newspapers lay blankets — moth-eaten, dingy and threadbare. Some were rolled together to make a pillow, the rest were interfolded to create a sort of sleeping bag. This was Luther's bed.

On the other side of the room, bricks had been stacked to support wooden planks of varying shapes and sizes and water-warped corrugated cardboard. On these shelves Luther kept his extra clothes, along with a thermos, a flashlight, a pile of tissue paper, another pile of folded tinfoil, some candle stubs, string and two partial books of matches. Assorted bottles and pop cans bulged from plastic grocery bags on the floor beneath the shelves.

The only other furniture was a makeshift table and a stool. The stool had three and a half legs. The missing portion of the fourth leg had been replaced with a gnarled tree branch butted to the broken leg and tied with string. The table base was a pair of rickety sawhorses. The tabletop had once been a small door. A round hole near one edge was all that remained of the doorknob, and into that Luther had stuffed a small can that held pencils, pens, a ruler and a pair of scissors.

Over half of the tabletop was covered with books. There were a few paperback novels, but most were hardcover texts with titles Nick could barely pronounce. Beside the books lay a small pile of paper. Unlike the tired appearance of everything else in the room, the paper was crisp and white, as if a spotlight were focused on it.

Nick rifled through the papers to see if Luther had written anything, but the pages were all blank. So far, Luther's hideaway told Nick nothing more than he already knew, and Nick began to lose heart. Perhaps there was no secret to Luther after all. Perhaps he was exactly what he appeared to be – a well-read vagrant with a surly nature and a sharp tongue who valued his privacy.

Then Nick noticed a small metal box, which he had overlooked because it was sandwiched among the stacked books. Carefully, he removed the books on top of it. The box had been bent, making the hinged lid difficult to open, but finally it popped free.

Inside was a gold pocket watch on a chain. Nick lifted it out and cradled it in his hand. It was icy cold and very heavy. It was magnificent – burnished gold with ornate scrollwork on its back and front. Nick snapped open the cover and studied the face of the watch inside. Elegant Roman numerals marked the hours, and hands resembling miniature wrought-iron arrows pointed out the time – 10:20. Nick checked his own watch. The time was correct. He had better hurry. As he was about to close the cover, he noticed an inscription. It read simply, *For Luther – Love always, Stefanie.*

Nick stared hard at the inscription to be sure his eyes weren't playing tricks on him. *For Luther – Love always, Stefanie.* He read it over and over. Nick closed the cover and toyed absently with the watch's chain. At last he had discovered something. He didn't know what it meant, but it was a start. Now he'd better get out before Luther returned.

As he went to replace the watch, Nick realized that the paper lining the bottom of the box wasn't just a piece of paper, but a photograph lying face down. With fingers clumsy from cold and nervousness, he lifted it out of the box and turned it over.

Smiling up at Nick was a woman in her early thirties and a boy a bit younger than himself. The woman had blonde hair, porcelain skin and laughing blue eyes. Her features were delicate, especially her mouth, but her eyes were full of mischief, and Nick felt happy looking at her. The boy looked much like the woman – same hair, same nose, same smile. Just the eyes were different – almost black.

Nick stared at the photograph, trying to memorize the faces. Then, reluctantly, he returned the snapshot and the watch to the metal box and shut the lid. He placed the box back in the stack of books, careful to leave everything exactly as he had found it. Then he backed out of the room and pulled the door shut until he heard the latch click.

He was afraid to turn around. He was afraid he would see Luther standing in the hall, watching him, knowing what he'd done, and hating him for it. It was so cold in the house that Nick could see his breath, yet his nervousness had Nick sweating. As quickly as he could, he tore down the stairs and headed for the kitchen. He would wait for Luther there.

The next half hour was torture. Try as he might, Nick couldn't get the photograph and watch out of his mind. He felt so guilty, he was sure Luther would know what he'd done the instant he saw his face.

When eleven o'clock arrived and Luther still hadn't shown up, Nick was relieved. His mother and Cole were expecting him by 11:30, and the walk home would take Nick almost half an hour. He couldn't stay any longer. He thought about leaving Luther the newspaper and the thermos of hot chocolate he'd brought, but changed his mind. Today, Nick would rather Luther think that he had never been there.

CHAPTER XII

B Y THE FOLLOWING FRIDAY, NICK'S GUILTY
conscience had all but disappeared. He had convinced himself that no harm had been done and that
his snooping might actually help Luther. Just the
same, he had no intention of letting Luther find out
about it.

He wished he understood the meaning of the
photograph and the pocket watch. Could these really
be the only things Luther had to show for his life?
Maybe they were just things he had found, like all the
other things he had stored in his locked room. But
Nick couldn't believe that. Luther's name was
engraved on the watch – it had to be his. And why
would anyone keep a snapshot of strangers? No, the
photograph and the watch were somehow linked
to Luther – and to each other. Nick was sure of it.

Perhaps the woman in the photograph was Stefanie,
the one who had given Luther the watch. Was the
boy her son? And how were they connected to

Luther? Was the woman his wife? His daughter? A friend?

The woman and boy had been well dressed, and the watch was obviously expensive. If these people were close to Luther, and if the watch was his, Luther hadn't always been a vagrant. So what happened?

Nick imagined all sorts of explanations. Luther had been mugged and knocked unconscious. When he'd come to, his memory was gone, and all he had left were the watch and the snapshot. Now he wandered the streets, hoping one day to find his identity.

Or maybe, Nick thought, the woman was Luther's greedy stepsister. Her father had married Luther's mother, a wealthy widow. Once he had control of her fortune, he'd committed her to an institution and kicked Luther into the street without a penny. His only reminders of that life were the watch, which had been a gift from his mother, and the snapshot of the stepsister he hoped to get even with one day.

There were so many possibilities, but not enough clues. Somehow, without Luther becoming suspicious, Nick was going to have to pump him for more information.

In the meantime, it was only a week until Christmas, and Nick was getting excited. School was out, so Nick's mother was home, flitting from room to room like a hummingbird, creating

Christmas magic. A wreath of pine cones welcomed visitors at the door. Pungent fir boughs and red velvet ribbons festooned the banisters leading upstairs. Pots of poinsettias cheered the hallway, and glorious kitchen smells danced with the traditional carols rising from the stereo.

Nick had always loved Christmas, but this year everything seemed more intense. When he walked through his front door, he could feel Christmas wrapping itself around him like a cat, warming him.

For the first time, Nick didn't concentrate on what he might get for Christmas. Instead, he was excited about the gifts he was planning to give. He'd been saving his allowance for months, and he knew exactly what he wanted to buy.

His mother had bought some silk flowers for her bedroom, and had been searching for the perfect container, but hadn't found it yet. Nick knew she admired a vase that their neighbor, Mrs. Muise, had in her home. Nick thought the vase was weird-looking, but his mother had gone on and on about how gorgeous it was. So Nick had asked Mrs. Muise where she'd bought it.

"Cairo," she said.

"Cairo?"

"Yes, Cairo." Then seeing how puzzled Nick looked, she added, "In Egypt. I bought it when I was on holiday."

"Oh," Nick sighed. There was no way he could go to Egypt to buy his mother a vase.

"Why do you ask, Nick?"

"Well, my mom really likes that vase, so I thought I'd buy her one like it for Christmas." He shrugged. "But I guess not. Oh well, I'll have to think of something else."

"Well, maybe not." Mrs. Muise smiled.

"What do you mean?"

"It just so happens that I've been thinking of replacing that vase. I've had it for quite a while, and it's time for a change."

"Really?"

"Um-hmm," Mrs. Muise nodded.

Nick couldn't believe his luck.

"Would you consider selling it?" he asked hopefully.

"Well, that depends. How much were you looking to spend?"

Nick did some mental math. What if the vase was too expensive? Finally he said, "I was hoping I could find something for about twenty-five dollars – plus tax, of course," he added hastily. "I guess I could go a bit higher …"

"You're in luck," Mrs. Muise interrupted. "The vase cost me about twenty dollars, and since it's been used and all, how about fifteen dollars – and no tax?"

"Are you serious?" Nick's eyes lit up.

"Absolutely," she smiled.

"Great! I'll go get my money. Don't sell it to anyone else before I get back."

"Hold on," Mrs. Muise laughed. "Christmas is still weeks away, and you don't want your mom finding her present. Why not leave the vase here until just before Christmas? You can pay me then. And I promise not to sell it to anyone else!"

"Great!" Nick beamed. "Thanks, Mrs. Muise. Thanks a lot."

Nick was also pleased with Cole's gift, though it also felt a bit strange. He knew Cole loved old sailing ships. He had books and books about them, and he even had some scale models, complete to the smallest detail. So when Nick saw a miniature ship-in-a-bottle paperweight, he knew it would be the perfect gift.

And that's what made him feel strange. He knew what Cole liked, and he was trying to please him. He could have bought him an ugly tie or polka-dotted socks, and Cole would have to thank him anyway. But this gift made Nick vulnerable. He wanted Cole to have it – and to like it – but part of him felt like he was going over to the enemy's side.

His gift for Luther, though, was the toughest. He could think of a hundred things Luther could use, but he didn't want to give him anything he needed. For one thing, he knew Luther would never accept it. No, he wanted to show Luther that he cared about him. But what would Luther like? What would he accept without taking offense?

What Nick really wanted was to bring Luther home with him. He hated the idea of Luther spending Christmas alone or having Christmas dinner at the House of Hope. But he knew that Luther would never come, and he would probably avoid Nick altogether if he suggested it.

He and Luther had agreed to meet at the McIntyre mansion on Wednesday, Christmas Eve. It was a glorious morning. Temperatures had risen and every snowdrift glittered like a hill of diamonds. As Nick tramped up the trail, a fluffy chickadee chirped at him from its perch on a nearby tree. Nick stopped to inhale the day and then felt in his pocket for the small square box.

Luther was waiting for Nick outside the house.

"I thought we might walk for a bit," he said. "It's too nice a day to be indoors."

So they threaded their way back down the trail, and then Luther led the way across Old Hill Road and into the woods on the other side. Nick was amazed at the number of pathways in an area no one used.

"Bet most people don't even know this place exists," Nick said.

Luther shrugged. "That's fine with me."

"Do these trails lead anywhere?" Nick asked.

Luther stopped walking and peered at Nick over his shoulder. "How long have you lived in this town, boy?"

"What are you saying?" Nick asked defensively.

"I'm saying that for a native of Andersonville, you don't seem to know a whole lot about it."

On they walked – Luther leading, Nick following dutifully behind. Finally Luther stopped, and Nick, who'd been studying the woods around him, walked right into him.

"Keep your eyes open!" Luther scowled.

"Sorry."

"Look over there." Luther pointed toward the trees ahead and slightly to his left. "What do you see?"

"Trees," Nick answered without hesitation.

Luther's arm fell lifelessly to his side and his shoulders sagged.

"Very good, Einstein. Do your powers of observation detect anything else?"

"You know, you're quite nasty sometimes," Nick pointed out, not the least bit bothered by Luther's sarcasm. "And that's not very good, especially at Christmas."

"My apologies," Luther said. "Santa might see me being naughty." They both knew he wasn't a bit sorry. "Can you see anything *among* the trees?"

"Yeah. I can see …"

"And don't tell me the sky and ground."

"Very funny." Nick squinted to bring meaning to the form he saw. "I'm not sure what it is. It looks like a roof, but it seems to be sitting on the ground."

"Well, well. I'm impressed. A roof it is, but it's not on the ground. Come on."

As they neared the roof, Nick realized he was seeing the top of a boathouse, and below, through the last of the trees, he saw the river, a ribbon of ice.

"Wow!" he exclaimed. "This is so cool! I didn't know the river flowed here. Hey, and look, Luther. There are stairs going down. Let's check 'em out."

Luther put a hand on Nick's arm.

"That's not a good idea. Those stairs haven't been used in years. There's no telling how safe they are."

"Oh, come on," Nick coaxed. "Is this part of the McIntyre property too?"

Luther nodded.

"Then I bet the stairs are just fine. Everything else they built is going to last forever."

"Ah, but in the spring, when the river is high, those stairs can be totally underwater, and water has a way of rotting wood."

"Oh, Luther, don't be an old stick-in-the-mud. Let's go and explore."

"Maybe another time — we'll come prepared to climb down safely."

"Ah, come on," Nick wheedled. "I'll go first."

"Mathew, don't push it! I said *no!*" Luther's command snapped sharply in the winter air.

"Pardon?" Nick stared at Luther. "What did you say?"

"I said *no.*" The urgency had left Luther's voice, but the authority was still there.

"You called me *Mathew.*"

"Did I? … Well, no matter. Next time I might call you George or Harry. Whatever your name is, we'd better head back. It's Christmas Eve, and I'm sure your family has plans."

They made their way back to Old Hill Road in silence.

"Well, have a good Christmas," Luther patted Nick on the shoulder and attempted a smile. Then he turned to leave.

"Wait," Nick said. "I have something for you."

Luther took a deep breath and then said flatly, "Nick, you know how I feel about you giving me things."

"Yeah, I know. But it's Christmas. Besides, it's not like I spent my college savings on you. Don't get all worked up. This present didn't cost me a cent. Not that I *wouldn't* have spent money on you," he added hastily, "but I already had this, and I thought it would be better for *you* to have it." With that, Nick removed a small gift-wrapped box from his pocket and offered it to Luther.

Luther didn't move.

"Go on, Luther," Nick said quietly. "It's Christmas. You have to accept it."

Reluctantly, Luther opened his hand, and Nick placed the box in it.

"I'll put it under the tree," Luther said gruffly.

"I'd like you to open it now," Nick said. "Please?"

Luther seemed to take forever unwrapping it, but at last he had the lid off the box and the silver chain in his hand.

"It's a St. Christopher's medal," Nick explained. "It's supposed to protect travelers."

"I know what it is," Luther said. "Where did you get it?"

"From my grandfather. He gave it to me when I was little. He said it would help me on my journey through life."

Luther nodded. "I appreciate the gesture, Nick, but I can't accept your gift."

"You *can*," Nick said belligerently. "What you're telling me is that you *won't*! You said no without even thinking. Well, I thought a long time about this. This medal is important to me, and I want you to have it."

For a few very long minutes they stood like statues in the middle of the road. Luther was the first to move. He studied Nick with piercing black eyes; then his eyebrows knit together and he grumbled,

"Then, thank you." And he slipped the chain over his head.

Nick's face lit up as though he'd been the one who'd just received a gift. "Great!" he grinned. "See you Saturday."

"Not so fast," Luther said. "You're not the only one who can give presents, you know."

"What?" Nick was instantly sober.

Luther reached into his parka and pulled out a flat rectangle wrapped roughly in tinfoil.

"For me?" Nick was astonished.

"What do you think?"

"Wow – I-I-I don't know what to say."

"Well, that's a first."

"What is it?" Nick asked excitedly.

"That would be telling."

"Can I open it now?"

"*May* I."

"*May* I open it now?"

"Of course not. Christmas is tomorrow. Now get home."

Nick smiled and Luther scowled.

"Thanks, Luther. And Merry Christmas."

"Hmmph."

Nick ran down Old Hill Road, waving wildly until Luther was no longer in sight, while Luther – fingering the medal around his neck – watched him go.

CHAPTER XIII

CHRISTMAS DAY WAS EVERYTHING NICK HAD HOPED it would be. His mother loved the vase and, before breakfast was even on the table, she had arranged the silk flowers in it. Seeing her so pleased sent warm shivers up Nick's spine, though he still thought the vase was weird.

Cole had been pleased with his gift too – and surprised. It was almost as though he'd been expecting an ugly tie or polka-dotted socks. He must have thanked Nick for the paperweight a dozen times, and more than once Nick had looked up to find Cole watching him curiously. They had both smiled uncomfortably and returned to what they'd been doing.

As for the gifts he'd been given, Nick liked them all because he hadn't had his heart set on anything.

Nick kept Luther's gift until last and opened it in his room. He hadn't placed it under the tree – he wouldn't have known how to explain it to his mom and Cole.

The tinfoil wasn't taped or tied, so the gift opened easily. It was obviously one of Luther's finds, and it had seen better days. The frame was pulling apart at the corners and the paint had rubbed off in several places. The glass was intact though, except for a crack near one corner. But what was inside the frame was unbelievable.

It was a drawing – a cartoon actually, but there was no doubt it was Nick. He was dressed in makeshift armor, and he was wearing gum boots. He held a garbage can lid as a shield in one hand and a bathroom plunger in the other. He was standing on the porch of the McIntyre mansion with the old hill falling away on both sides of him. On the shield, *Nick the Conqueror* had been written in calligraphy, and at the bottom of the picture it read, *Plunge on!*

As Nick studied the drawing more closely, he saw that the hillside was strewn with all the things he had experienced with Luther. There was a thorny bush with a shoe snagged on it and a grammar book open beside it. There were kids playing keep-away with a glove and a boy stuffed awkwardly into a trash can. There was the security guard from the Capizzi Center and Luther's wire cart. There was a flashlight and police officers. There was lightning and snow. They were so cleverly drawn it was impossible to take them all in. Every time Nick looked at the picture, he saw something new.

It was just an ink sketch with pencil crayon accents, but the likenesses and detail were amazing. This was a work of art, and the artist's signature was in the corner.

Maybe he would discover Luther's identity at last. The writing was hard to read, but Nick studied it eagerly. Yes, there was *Luther* – with an oversized *L*. The last name began with a huge swishy *S*. Nick peered closely at the rest of it. He couldn't make out any of the letters except for another huge letter – a *C* – in the middle. What had Luther called himself – *Luther Sincere*? Was that the name he'd signed? If so, why the large *C*?

Nick scratched his head. He'd never seen this drawing before, but he knew the style. He knew the signature too – even if he couldn't read it. It was just beyond his memory's grasp, but it would come to him, he told himself. He was gathering more clues all the time. Soon they would all fall into place.

Cole had been right about Nick's mother. Her morning sickness had passed and she was her cheerful self once more. She had roses in her cheeks and a bounce in her step. With less than four months until the baby was due, she also had an expanding waistline.

They hadn't talked much about the baby since Nick had run away, but Nick realized his mother and Cole probably didn't want to upset him again. He was past the shock, but what he wanted now was to understand how a new baby was going to change things.

Cole was at the newspaper, and Nick's mother was knitting. If he wanted answers, now was as good a time as any. He took a deep breath.

"Mom?"

"Um-hmm?" she answered without looking up.

"Is that for the baby?"

She smiled at Nick and held up her work for him to see.

"Yes. It's going to be a sweater, a bonnet and booties. Here's a picture of what it should look like when it's finished. That's what I'll put on the baby when we bring it home from the hospital."

"What if it's a boy?"

"It's yellow, so it's okay for a boy or a girl."

Nick wrinkled his nose.

"Isn't it kind of lacy-looking for a boy?"

"What would you prefer? A baseball cap, a sweatshirt and runners?"

"Yeah."

She laughed again. "All in good time."

"What are you going to call it?"

"We've sort of been thinking of Blaize if it's a girl. What do you think?"

"Blaize? It sounds like a horse."

His mother chuckled. "I guess it does. What about Jessica? Jess for short."

Nick shrugged. "It's better than Blaize, that's for sure. What about if it's a boy?"

"We don't know. The only thing for sure is that he can't be named Nicholas. Two Nicholas's are enough."

"Two?"

"Um-hmm. You and Cole. Your names are both short for Nicholas."

"Oh yeah?"

"Sure. Didn't you realize that, honey?"

Nick shook his head slowly. "Uh-uh. I thought Cole was just Cole. We have the same name, eh?"

His mother nodded. They were both quiet for a moment.

Nick said at last, "Lots of kids are named after their parents. Do you think Cole minds that he can't name his son after him?"

Nick's mother looked him straight in the eyes and said, "Not for a second."

Nick wasn't sure why, but he was relieved. Then he asked, "Where is the baby going to sleep?"

Nick's mother sighed.

"That's a good question. At first it can sleep in a cradle in Cole's and my room, but babies grow pretty fast, and it should have its own room."

Nick made a big decision. "It could share my room."

"Nick, that's really wonderful. You have no idea how happy your offer makes me. But babies don't keep the same hours as boys. It wouldn't work for either of you. No, I'm going to have to give up my sewing room – turn it into a nursery."

"But that's way at the other end of the hall from your room. And besides, you waited so long to get a sewing room."

"Oh, Nick, it's not such a big deal. Maybe Cole will turn the downstairs guest room into a sewing room for me. It's twice as big anyway."

"Hey, wait. I've got it," Nick beamed. "How about I move into the downstairs room, and the baby can have my room? That way the baby will be right across the hall from you, you'll get to keep your sewing room, and I won't wake up when it cries."

Nick's mother looked skeptical. "Are you sure you want to be downstairs all by yourself?"

"For Pete's sake, Mom. I'm almost thirteen years old!"

She winked at him. "So you are. I keep forgetting. Does that mean you're ready to pass on some of your kid stuff to your new brother or sister?"

"What stuff?"

"There are boxes and boxes of things in the attic. I packed them away years ago – clothes, books, toys, you name it."

"Really?" Nick grinned. "That's so neat. I didn't know you'd kept stuff. Let's check it out."

"Right this instant?"

Nick nodded. "Why not?"

Their afternoon in the attic was like a picnic. They brushed away the cobwebs, blew away the dust, and rediscovered the past.

"I wore a *dress*?" Nick demanded indignantly.

"It's a christening gown," his mother laughed.

"It's a dress," Nick insisted. "Give it to the baby for sure. And don't you dare tell anyone I ever wore that."

"It's too late," she chuckled. "All the relatives have pictures of you in it. And anyway, you were adorable."

"Mom!" Nick wailed.

"Well, it's true."

"What's in this one?" Nick asked, dragging out the next cardboard carton.

"Like I'm supposed to remember. Open it up and see."

"It's books," he announced, ripping open the top.

"Oh, Nick, all your baby books. Look at these." She pulled out some cloth books and other books with thick cardboard pages. "You used to eat the stories instead of read them."

"No wonder," he said. "There's not a lot here.

'*Bow-wow* says the dog. *Moo* says the cow.' Great stuff, Mom."

She cuffed his ear. "Don't get smart. Nobody starts with *War and Peace*. Oh, look, Nick! *The Pokey Little Puppy*. Do you remember that?"

Nick shook his head, but his mother didn't seem to notice. "Oh, wow! *Bambi* and *Sleeping Beauty*. You used to call it Sleeping Booby. Oh, and Nick, look! It's *Alexander's Terrible, Horrible, No-good, Very Bad Day*. You must remember that one! It was one of your favorites. The only one you liked better was *The Adventures of Jeremy Jones*."

Nick slipped his thumbs through his belt loops and drawled, "*Well, I'll be a mud-slidin', turtle-ridin', iceberg-climbin', blue-bell-chimin'* ..." and then his mother joined him "... *son of a yodeler in the Swiss Alps*." They burst out laughing.

"Is that in here?" Nick asked.

"Oh, it must be. I can't imagine throwing it out. That one and *Arnie Aardvark Hates Ants* and *Mrs. Meeker's Monsters* – you never got tired of those books. You adored anything by Luther St. Cyr."

Nick's head shot up. That was it! That was Luther's name – Luther *St. Cyr*! Not Luther *Sincere*. Of course! That's why Luther had made a joke out of his last name. He did it to put Nick off.

He ploughed through the box, searching for Luther's books. There they were, and they were so familiar. It was Luther all right. The pictures were all done in the same unmistakable style, and the signature was the same too – *Luther St. Cyr* – scrawled in the corner of each drawing. Now that he knew what it said, he didn't have any trouble reading Luther's signature.

But as he flipped through the books, a scary thought struck him. His Luther – *Luther St. Cyr* – was a famous author and illustrator. *And* he was a vagrant in Andersonville.

CHAPTER XIV

BACK IN HIS OWN ROOM, NICK COMPARED THE illustrations in the books with the sketch Luther had given him for Christmas. Carefully, he examined sketch after sketch, signature after signature. With each drawing, he was more and more awed by Luther's talent.

It didn't make sense. Why would Luther walk away from a successful career to live on the streets? It just wasn't a logical choice unless ... *unless he'd* had *no choice.* That had to be it. Luther must have been forced to give up his other life, just like Mac, the boy in the soup kitchen. But why? What could make him do that?

Nick flipped to the back flap of one of the books, where there was a photograph and biography of the author. But when he saw the glossy snapshot, his hopes fell. It wasn't Luther after all.

Then Nick looked more closely. The book had to be ten years old, which meant the photograph would also be at least that old. He tried to picture Luther younger and clean shaven, with a haircut and in a suit – and smiling.

Nick read the blurb beneath the picture.

Luther St. Cyr, a long-time editor with Pollyanna Press, began his career as a writer ten years ago when his son was born. His books won instant acceptance with children everywhere. Since the publication of his first book, Simon Says, *Luther has never looked back.*

His simple but captivating tales have won the hearts of children and adults alike, and his vivid, detailed illustrations are delightful fantasies.

Luther St. Cyr lives outside Toronto with his wife and son.

"With his wife and son," Nick repeated aloud as if in a trance. What wife and son? The people in the photograph in the bent metal box? *Was that Stefanie?*, Nick wondered. Was the boy Luther's son? The boy was so much like the woman, but he had piercing black eyes – like Luther's, Nick realized suddenly.

Nick flipped to the front of the book. There it was, the copyright date. It had been published eleven years ago. Nick dug through the pile strewn on his bed until he found Luther's first book, *Simon Says*. Then he turned to its copyright page. It was eighteen years old. If Luther had started writing when his son was born, that would make his son about eighteen or nineteen years old. Yet the boy in the photograph had looked about ten. Perhaps he wasn't Luther's son.

Nick turned the page and stopped. Then he flipped through all the books as fast as he could, looking for the dedication in each one. Just as he had suspected, it was always the same. *For Mathew.*

What did it all mean? Nick tried to sort it out. First of all, Luther was a successful author. Second, he had a wife and son. Third, Luther had dedicated all his books to Mathew, the name he had called Nick by in the woods. Last, Luther lived as a vagrant.

With each new piece of information came more questions. Where were Luther's wife and son? When had Luther written his last book? Why was Luther living as a bum?

If the sketch he had given Nick for Christmas was any indication, Luther certainly hadn't lost his skill. Nick remembered the pile of white paper in Luther's room. Was Luther writing and living as a bum at the same time?

The key to the mystery had to be Luther's wife and son. Who were they? *Where* were they? Nick needed answers – and he certainly couldn't ask Luther.

When Nick's mother went to the library the next day, Nick tagged along. Using the computer, he searched for titles by Luther St. Cyr. The computer listed only the books Nick already had at home. That wasn't a surprise. As far back as Nick could remember, Luther had been a vagrant in Andersonville.

Now what? If Luther had been a successful writer, there must be more information on him somewhere. But where?

"Excuse me," he said to the librarian. "Could you please tell me where to find information about somebody famous?"

The librarian smiled. "Did you have someone particular in mind?"

Nick wasn't sure if he should tell. But he decided that the librarian was probably too busy to care why Nick wanted to find out about Luther. So he said, "Luther St. Cyr – the writer."

"Have you tried the *Who's Who?*"

"What's that?" Nick asked.

"Come on. I'll show you."

Luther wasn't mentioned in the current edition or in the one before it. Nick had to dig back nine years before he found Luther listed. His eyes gobbled up the information. Luther had been a university scholar, with a whole list of academic honors. Hah! Nick had known all along that Luther was intelligent. He had also been a competitive swimmer, earning himself a spot on the national team. Was there nothing Luther couldn't do?

Nick read on.

The biography described Luther's career as an editor and then his overnight success as an author and illustrator. Then it gave some of Luther's personal history. He had been born in a small Ontario town, the only child of Anna and Emile St. Cyr, who had owned a bookstore. So that's where Luther's love of books came from!

Then came the big surprise. According to the *Who's Who*, Luther was only forty-nine years old. Nick had always thought of Luther as being really old, but forty-nine wasn't all that ancient. Heck, it was only about ten years older than Cole. No wonder Nick hadn't recognized Luther's photograph on the book jacket. In the last ten years he must have aged thirty, Nick thought. Since seeing the people on Hope Avenue, he had no doubt that life on the streets could do that to a person.

He returned to his reading. "Luther is a devoted family man. When he isn't writing, he spends his time with his wife Stefanie and his ten-year-old son Mathew."

Nick slapped the page. The photograph in the bent metal box had to be of Stefanie and Mathew. It was a ten-year-old photograph of Luther's wife and son.

An uncomfortable knot tightened in the pit of Nick's stomach. Every clue he uncovered seemed to hit a wall, a ten-year-old wall. It was almost as though Luther's life had stopped ten years ago.

"Ready to go?"

Nick nearly jumped out of his chair.

"Sorry," his mother chuckled, placing a hand on Nick's shoulder. "I didn't mean to startle you. What's got you so preoccupied? More research for your report?" she asked, looking down at the book. "Oh, Luther St. Cyr. Why the sudden interest?"

Nick shrugged.

"Just curious. Those old books in the attic – they're still fun. I wanted to see if he'd written anything lately. But you know, Mom, he hasn't written anything in ten years. Why would anyone that talented suddenly just stop doing what he's good at?"

"I don't know. It doesn't say?"

Nick shook his head. "No. The newest information is ten years old. It's like he suddenly fell off the planet."

"Maybe he's dead."

"No, he's alive," Nick said too quickly.

His mother eyed him quizzically. "How can you be so sure?"

Nick had to think fast.

"Well, if he'd died, they would have included him one last time in an obituary. So he must be alive."

"That makes sense," his mother conceded. "Hmm. It does make you wonder, doesn't it? Just think of all the books he hasn't written. Now you've got me curious. Why don't you ask Cole about it? I bet the newspaper has all kinds of connections. If anyone can find out, Cole can."

Not long ago, Nick would have had his jaw wired shut rather than ask Cole for a favor. It still felt awkward, but he needed answers, and his mother was right – Cole probably would be able to help.

He could have asked him at the dinner table – it would have been easier with his mother there – but something made him wait until later, when Cole was in the living room reading.

"Cole?" Nick began tentatively.

"Um-hmm," Cole answered, absorbed in his book.

"Have you got a second?"

Cole peered at Nick over his reading glasses. Then he removed them, closed his book and placed them both on the table beside him.

"You bet," he said. "What's on your mind? Your research project?"

Nick shook his head.

"Well, how's it going anyway?" Cole asked.

"Good, I guess. I'm nearly finished."

"You've worked really hard, Nick. You should be proud. I'd love to read it when you're done. Would you mind?"

Nick smiled sheepishly.

"No problem."

Cole cleared his throat. "Great. But, um, that's not what you're here about. What can I do for you?"

Nick took a deep breath and began.

"Well, you know how Mom and I were up in the attic yesterday, going through my old baby stuff?"

Cole grinned. "Your mom showed me your dress."

"Jeez!" Nick fumed, but he wasn't really angry. "I told her not to tell anyone."

"She was excited," Cole shrugged. "I think it just sort of slipped out."

"Anyway, while we were up there, we found all my old books. I'd forgotten most of them, but Mom hadn't. She gushed over everything – you know what she's like."

"Oh, yes."

"But I did remember some of the books, especially the ones by Luther St. Cyr."

"I don't know them."

"Hang on a sec," Nick said. "I'll show you." Nick was upstairs and down again in thirty seconds. He plunked the books in Cole's lap.

Cole put his glasses on, and Nick held his breath while Cole studied the books.

"I can see why you would remember these," Cole said. "They're terrific, particularly the artwork. This man has quite a talent."

"Well, that's the thing." Nick forgot his awkwardness as he became more involved with his story.

"Today when Mom and I went to the library, I tried to find some more books. There weren't any. I have all the books he's ever written, and the newest one is ten years old. So then I looked him up in the *Who's Who* and ..."

"You did?" Cole smiled. "You're getting to be quite the detective. You have the makings of a really good investigative reporter. Maybe you should come and work for me down at the paper."

Nick grinned self-consciously. "Well ... the librarian gave me the idea. But anyway, the *Who's Who* hasn't included anything about Luther in ten years."

"That's strange."

"Which is why I was wondering if you know some way I could find out what's happened to him."

"Right. The easiest thing would be to ask the publisher. Who is it, anyway?"

"Pollyanna Press," Nick blurted out. "So what do I do? Write them a letter?"

Cole was thoughtful for a few seconds.

"You could do that, though it might take a while to get an answer. Publishing houses are busy places, and ten years is a long time. There may not be anyone there who remembers Luther St. Cyr."

"You're kidding!" Nick's dismay showed clearly on his face.

"It's just a possibility," Cole backpedaled. "But you'll never know until you try. Look, what if I fax the publisher — sort of like official business from the newspaper? I might get some action a little faster."

"You'd do that?"

"No problem. First thing tomorrow morning. Okay?"

"Okay. And thanks."

CHAPTER XV

THE NEXT MORNING NICK COMPLETED HIS REPORT for school. Just like Cole working on an article for the newspaper, Nick shut himself up in the study behind the computer, with his research notes spread out around him.

Once he'd finished, Nick couldn't tell if his report was good or bad. He couldn't see the people he'd met as just "a problem" anymore. They were people like him, like Luther.

Luther! He'd been the reason Nick had done the report in the first place, but there was nothing about Luther in it. Nick had made sure of that. What he had learned from Luther would have made his report better, but that would betray his trust. And Nick couldn't do that.

While the computer checked his spelling and printed the report, Nick studied the ship-in-a-bottle paperweight he'd given Cole for Christmas. He caught himself smiling, and even though he was alone, he felt silly. Then, fastening the pages of his report with a paper clip, Nick slipped it into a file folder with the pictures he'd taken and pushed it to the side of the desk. He was done.

The rest of the day dragged by for Nick. He was restless and couldn't sit still even to watch television or play video games. He couldn't concentrate. When his mother beat him four games in a row at Chinese checkers, she knew something was wrong.

"What's the matter with you, Nick? The lights are on, but nobody's home, and you're fidgeting as if you just sat on an anthill. I think you've had too much Christmas vacation. It's time to go back to school."

"Nice try, Mom."

"Well, it's time for something. You've been in the house all day. Why not get your skates and hockey stick and go over to the rink?"

But even hockey didn't shake Nick out of his mood, and his friends didn't coax him to stay when he left the ice in the middle of the game.

All he could think about was Luther. Would Cole come home with some answers? Would Cole even remember to ask?

Nick thought about phoning him at work to remind him, but that would make him seem too anxious. He couldn't let Cole or his mother know how important the information was to him.

Maybe Cole wouldn't be able to get any information. Maybe Pollyanna Press would ignore his fax. Maybe no one there would remember Luther. Maybe they had closed down.

But Nick was just as afraid that Cole *would* get answers. When he thought about the facts he had, Nick couldn't imagine that the missing puzzle pieces could be anything but bad news. Yet once he had the whole story, no matter how awful it was, Nick was certain he'd be able to help Luther.

When Cole finally arrived home from work, Nick's anxiety grew. Like Nick, Cole seemed preoccupied, and dinner was very quiet. Nick tried to look normal. He cut his food and ate it a forkful at a time, like he did every meal. But he didn't taste any of it and, afterward, he couldn't remember what he'd eaten. Nick's stomach was churning – he wanted to shake Cole until he got the information. Though Cole hadn't said anything, Nick was sure that he had asked and that he had answers. But if Nick didn't get them soon, he was going to burst. His mother made a few attempts at conversation, but realized she was fighting a losing battle and gave up.

"I'll clean up," she announced when the meal was finally over. "Why don't you two go spread your sunshine somewhere else? It's selfish of me to keep it all to myself."

Cole squeezed her shoulder and gave her a peck on the cheek.

"Sorry, Carol," he apologized. "I guess I wasn't very good company."

"Oh, really? I hadn't noticed." Then she smiled and swatted him with the tea towel. "Go on. Get out of here – both of you."

Cole turned to Nick and shrugged. "I think she's trying to get rid of us. Let's go see if there's a hockey game on the tube."

With the T.V. going, Cole said quietly, "I faxed Pollyanna Press this morning."

"Oh, yeah?" Nick tried to sound casual.

"Yeah."

"Any luck?"

"Not until about 3:30. Then I got a phone call from a Ms. Johnson, one of the editors. Apparently, she worked with St. Cyr on all his books. She says they were friends."

Nick didn't like the way Cole said *were*. It sounded as if Luther was dead.

"And?" he said hopefully. "She must have been able to tell you something, right?"

"Quite a lot, actually." Cole looked Nick in the eyes and frowned. "I'm afraid it's not good news, Nick."

"Oh." Nick didn't know what else to say.

"Remember how you said Luther St. Cyr just seemed to vanish about ten years ago?"

Nick nodded.

"Well, that's exactly what happened."

"But *why?*" Nick's impatience was getting the best of him. "Did she say *why?*"

"Ms. Johnson said St. Cyr was always a pretty serious fellow – likable enough, but gruff, hard to get close to – until he met and married his wife."

"Stefanie."

"Yes, Stefanie. Well, apparently Stefanie was able to unlock a lighter, happier side of Luther that no one had ever seen. He became more outgoing. He became more friendly to his co-workers. In fact, according to Ms. Johnson, he became quite a practical joker. He also became quite stylish, wearing three-piece suits that had to be seen to be believed. In his vest pocket he always kept a gold pocket watch his wife had given him as a wedding present. Ms. Johnson said his face would light up whenever anyone asked him for the time, and he would make a big production of pulling out his watch and popping open the cover."

And now that watch sat in a battered metal box, Nick thought glumly.

"About four years after Stefanie and Luther were married, their son Mathew was born," Cole continued. "Luther was over the moon: the sun rose and set on Mathew. That's when he started writing. No one at Pollyanna Press had any idea he was so talented. Ms. Johnson said his stories were natural kid-catchers and his illustrations were magical. They'd never seen anything quite like it. Luther's work was unique – and Pollyanna struck it rich. As fast as he could complete the books, they were on the bookstands."

"So what went wrong?"

"I'm getting there. Trust me, it's important to hear everything."

Nick took a deep breath and tried to relax.

"The St. Cyrs bought a big old house in a small town outside Toronto, and that's where Luther did his writing – so he could be near his family. They also had a cottage on a lake. Both Luther and Stefanie were great outdoor people – they loved hiking and boating and swimming. So their cottage was perfect."

Nick was sitting ramrod straight, his fists clenched tightly on his knees.

"Anyway, it all fell to pieces when Mathew was about ten. It was June and school had just finished, so the family was preparing for a summer at the lake. Luther was putting the finishing touches on his latest book, but one illustration was driving him crazy. To anyone else, it looked perfect, but he wouldn't hand it in to Ms. Johnson until he was happy with it. Mathew was chomping at the bit to get to the lake, and Luther couldn't concentrate. Feeling guilty about holding up the family holiday, Luther sent Stefanie and Mathew on ahead. He'd finish up the drawing and meet them at the lake in two days."

"And did he?" Nick asked, hoping against hope, but already knowing the answer.

"Ms. Johnson was at Luther's house collecting the finished manuscript when the police arrived. There had been a swimming accident – both Stefanie and Mathew had drowned."

Nick turned white.

"Are you all right, Nick? You look like you're going to be sick. I'm sorry. I know this is horrible."

"No, I'm okay. Go on."

Cole seemed reluctant to continue.

"Please, Cole. Just finish."

"Ms. Johnson said that after the accident, Luther kept blaming himself. *If he had gone with them, if he hadn't sent them on ahead, if he hadn't been so picky about the art* – any way he looked at it, he felt their deaths were his fault. And time didn't help; if anything, it made things worse. He wouldn't allow that last book to be published. When he spoke at all, he was surly. He stopped eating. He stopped paying attention to his appearance. He locked himself up in his house and wouldn't let anyone in except Ms. Johnson. She said it was as though he had died with Stefanie and Mathew."

Nick's heart ached for Luther.

"Then one day, Luther disappeared. Ms. Johnson went to check on him and found the front door wide open. It was as though he'd been beamed aboard a spaceship by aliens. He didn't leave a letter, and he took nothing with him. Not even money. His wallet with all his identification and credit cards was still on his dresser, and his car was in the garage."

"Just the watch and a picture," Nick muttered.

"Pardon?"

"Sorry. Nothing." Nick was so caught up in his own thoughts, he had forgotten Cole was there.

"So that's the whole sad story," Cole sighed, "except ..."

"Except what?" Nick asked sharply, and Cole looked at him strangely.

"Except that he's been missing so long now that he's been declared legally dead. All his possessions — his house, furniture, car, investments — everything has been sold, and the money has been given to his next of kin, some distant cousin. The only thing left is the book that he was working on. Ms. Johnson kept it. Apparently, she doesn't believe that Luther's dead, which is all well and good, except that nobody knows where he is."

"No. Nobody knows," Nick repeated quietly.

"Ms. Johnson wanted to know why I was so curious

about Luther."

Nick looked up. "What did you tell her?"

Cole shrugged. "I said you were a big fan and were wondering why there hadn't been any Luther St. Cyr books in years."

"Did she believe you?"

Cole seemed puzzled.

"Why wouldn't she?"

CHAPTER XVI

NICK WAS ALL MIXED UP. HE HAD BEEN CERTAIN HE could help Luther if he just knew the truth about him. But now he had the truth – Luther's family was gone – and there was nothing he could do about it. Could Nick get Luther to see that life was still good? *Was* it good?

It was the last Saturday before school started. Nick was on his way to the McIntyre mansion, but he was dreading it. He knew he was going to tell Luther everything – he couldn't hold it inside. Luther would guess something was wrong, so he might as well come right out with it.

He had no idea how Luther would react. He would be hurt, Nick was sure of that. How could he not be? But Luther would probably mask his hurt with anger. Nick was used to Luther's gruffness. He had learned that Luther's snide comments and cold manner were just armor. They didn't keep Luther from feeling, they just allowed him to pretend he didn't feel. But what would Luther do *after* his anger? That was the scary part.

As usual, Nick found Luther in the kitchen, sitting on the floor.

"Well, if that's not the longest face I've ever seen, I don't know what is," Luther greeted him. "You look like you swallowed Scrooge."

Nick attempted a weak smile.

"Come now. You go back to school on Monday, but it's not exactly the death penalty."

Nick shook his head. "It's not that."

"Problems at home?" Luther was serious now.

Nick was thoughtful for a few seconds, and then he said, "No. Actually, things at home are sort of okay."

"Well, I'm glad to hear that," Luther said, and Nick could tell he meant it. "But something's bothering you. Now if you don't want to talk about it, just say so."

"It's you!" Nick blurted.

"What's me?"

"You're what's bothering me."

"Why? What did I do?"

"I know who you are."

"Well, good for you. Considering I told you who I am, you'll excuse me if I don't turn cartwheels in recognition of your brilliance."

"No, Luther. I mean it. I've known all along you aren't a bum."

"Then you're even more stupid than you look, because a bum is exactly what I am."

"No, you're not."

"Yes, I am. Now let's just drop the subject."

But now that he'd started, Nick was determined to get everything off his chest.

"You're not Luther *Sincere*. You're Luther *St. Cyr*, the author and illustrator. I have every book you've ever written."

"Not quite," Luther muttered, but Nick heard him.

"That's true. There's one that hasn't been published."

Luther's eyes narrowed. Nick waited for him to explode, but he didn't.

"May I ask how you come to know so much about me?"

"A bit by accident and the rest by digging."

"I see. And would it be asking too much for you to tell me exactly what you've found out?"

So Nick told him. He told him the whole story, beginning with the Christmas sketch and ending with Cole's conversation with Ms. Johnson. The only thing he left out was the day he'd gone exploring in Luther's room.

Luther listened, his face expressionless. When Nick was finished, a heavy silence fell over the room.

When he couldn't stand it any longer, Nick

demanded, "Aren't you going to say something?"

Luther raised his eyes, but he wasn't looking at Nick. It was more like he was looking through him, beyond him. At last his gaze focused, but there was no anger there. The naked pain Nick saw ripped at his heart. And he hated himself for causing it.

After a time, Luther slowly looked away and, in an empty voice, said, "Go home, Nick."

All that day, during the long night that followed and throughout the next day, guilt, sadness and worry played tag inside Nick's head. He was drowning in emotions bigger than he was. He wanted to run to his mother for comfort, like a little boy, but he knew she couldn't make it all better. No one could.

What business did he have interfering? What business did he have snooping in Luther's life? How could he have thought he could solve Luther's problems? Heck, he couldn't even solve his own! He was so stupid! If he'd just accepted Luther as he was, Luther wouldn't be so hurt right now.

But he *was* hurt. Every time Nick shut his eyes, he saw Luther as he had seen him last – an empty man. Nick could deal with Luther being angry. But the Luther Nick kept seeing in his mind was without hope, and it broke Nick's heart.

When Nick had left Luther, he'd been a sagging heap on the kitchen floor. What if he hadn't moved? What if he was so trapped by his memories that he couldn't move? If he didn't move, he would freeze to death!

And it would all be Nick's fault.

By Sunday evening, Nick had dark circles under his eyes from lack of sleep and his head was pounding. Passing him headache tablets and a glass of water, his mother laid a hand on his forehead.

"Well, you don't have a fever, Nick, but you look awful and you're as pale as can be. I sure hope you're not coming down with something."

Nick forced a smile he didn't feel.

"I'm okay, Mom. I just didn't sleep very well last night, and I have a headache." It was the truth, as far as it went.

His mother studied him earnestly. "I wonder why."

Nick shrugged. "Maybe I'm just excited about going back to school."

"Uh-huh. And I'm Snow White." Then she said more seriously, "Are you sure there isn't something you want to talk about, Nick?"

"Like what?" Nick was sincerely puzzled. "Not the birds and bees stuff again, Mom, please."

She smiled. "No. I was thinking more about things here at home. Are you still upset about Cole and the baby? If that's what's bothering you, maybe we should talk about it."

"No, Mom, I'm not upset about that anymore. The baby's cool. It'll take a bit of getting used to, but I'm okay about it. Who knows? I might even like the little sucker, as long as you don't call it Blaize."

They both smiled.

"And Cole?" his mother asked hopefully.

Nick hated to admit it, but he didn't really mind Cole at all anymore.

"He's okay," he mumbled. "Anyway, he's the baby's father, so I guess we've gotta keep him, right?"

His mother kissed the top of his head.

"Have I ever told you what a wonderful kid you are?"

"Does that mean I get a raise in my allowance?"

"Not a chance. Now get to bed. You need a good night's sleep."

He did need a good night's sleep, but he didn't get it. He spent the night torturing himself with thoughts of Luther, and when he finally drifted off, he dreamt of Luther in the McIntyre place, slowly freezing to death. In his dream, Nick tried to rouse Luther – he shook him and shouted at him – but Luther didn't move. He didn't even see Nick. He just sat there, getting cold and stiff.

"Nick, wake up. It's okay. It's okay. It's only a dream." Cole was shaking him.

"Luther! Where's Luther? Is he okay?" Nick was disoriented. He was sweating and every muscle in his body was tight.

"Relax, Nick. You were having a nightmare," Cole soothed him. "You're okay now. Just relax."

Little by little, Nick's body started to unknot. He pushed himself up to a sitting position.

"I'm hot. I need a drink of water. Where's Mom?"

"She's sleeping. I was working and I heard you yelling." He smiled. "But you're fine now, Nick. It was only a bad dream. I'll get you some water. Hang on. I'll be right back."

Cole returned with the water and a cold cloth. Beneath the cool, soothing touch of the cloth, the tension left Nick's body and, at last, he slept.

CHAPTER XVII

WHEN NICK AWOKE THE NEXT MORNING, COLE HAD already left for work. Nick's mother eyed him with concern.

"I don't know, Nick. You just don't look well. And Cole said you had a nightmare last night. Maybe you should stay home today and try to get some rest."

"Mom, I'm okay," Nick insisted, though he still had a fierce headache and he was exhausted. "It was just a dream. I'll live. I don't want to miss the first day. Really, I'm fine."

His mother looked doubtful.

"Well, all right, I guess. But I'm worried about you. If you find the day is too much, just call me or Cole to pick you up. Okay?"

Nick nodded. "Okay."

But Nick had no intention of going to school – not right away, anyhow. First he had to find Luther. He didn't expect Luther to forgive him for what he'd done, but he had to make sure he was safe. He would never make it through another day not knowing how Luther was.

"Let me drive you, then," Nick's mother interrupted his thoughts. "It's really cold."

"Mom, you're fussing for nothing," Nick protested, alarmed by this sudden hitch in his plan. Then he lied. "Besides, I told Josh I'd see him on the bus. We're both taking the eight o'clock Ramsey Avenue Express."

"Why so early? School doesn't start until nine."

"I know, but we're going in to help set up for an assembly." Nick couldn't believe how easily the lies came.

"Oh? You never mentioned that before."

"I guess I forgot."

"Well, don't overexert yourself."

"I won't, I promise." At least that part was true, he consoled himself.

As Nick stood on the street waiting for the bus, he knew, without looking, that his mother was watching him from the living room window. Thank goodness the bus was on time. Nick gave the driver his fare and took a seat near the rear door. Two stops later, he pulled the cord and got off. Now his walk was even longer, but he couldn't afford to let his mother suspect anything. Quickly, he veered off Ramsey Avenue and jogged in the opposite direction, toward the McIntyre mansion.

It was so cold that Nick's cheekbones ached, and he pulled his scarf up over his nose. Again and again he inhaled the same stale air, but at least it was warm and moist. Besides, concentrating on breathing took his mind off his watering eyes. But nothing could stop him from thinking about Luther. In a way, he hoped he wouldn't be at the McIntyre place. He hoped Luther had snapped out of his stupor and gone to the Beacon Mission – at least he'd be warm there.

Nick plodded along Old Hill Road – his feet had gone numb four blocks ago. Clumsily, he zigzagged his way up the trail and let himself in the side door. Frantically calling Luther's name, Nick half-ran, half-tripped from room to room, desperately searching for any sign of his friend. When he reached the second floor landing and saw the door to the locked room wide open, Nick knew Luther was gone – not just to the shelter, but gone for good.

The note on the table confirmed it.

Sunday, January 4

Dear Nick,

Don't feel bad. You did nothing wrong. You just made me face what I've known for quite a while. It's time for me to move on.

Your friend,
Luther

KRISTIN BUTCHER

A lump the size of a large rock lodged itself in Nick's throat, and burning tears filled his eyes. Luther was running away again. Now that Nick had put all the pieces together, Luther felt cornered. The only thing Nick's prying had managed to do was to drive Luther away.

Nick tossed Luther's books every which way. *Where was it? Where was the box?* Finally, he spied it sitting open on Luther's bed. It was empty.

He picked up a book and heaved it against the wall with all his might. Then he crumpled to the floor and buried his face in his arms.

After a while, he realized he wasn't alone.

"Tell me what's wrong, Nick," a voice urged gently. "Maybe I can help."

Nick recognized the voice. He shook his head without looking up.

"It's too late!" he sobbed into his arms. "Nobody can help now. He's gone and it's all my fault."

Cole hunkered down and put a comforting arm around Nick's shoulders.

"Luther?" he asked.

Nick lifted his head and nodded.

"Nick, this Luther ... your friend ... is he the same Luther who's one of Andersonville's better-known vagrants?"

Nick nodded again.

"And is he also the author you've been researching?"

"Yes," Nick squeaked, taking a deep breath and wiping his eyes.

"And is this where you've been spending your Saturday mornings?"

"Uh-huh."

"This is beginning to make sense. Now tell me why you think he's gone."

Nick still held the note crumpled tightly in his hand. He passed it to Cole, but before Cole could read it, Nick was shouting.

"And now he's out on some highway somewhere in the middle of winter, and no one will give him a ride because he's a bum, and he's going to freeze, and he'll die, and it's all my fault!"

Cole finished reading the note and gave Nick's shoulder a squeeze. Then he said firmly, "Nothing is your fault, and Luther's not going to die." He paused and then added, "Because we're going to find him."

Nick was shocked into silence for a moment. Then, "We are?" he asked hopefully.

"We are," Cole confirmed. "But first, we've got to get you warmed up. You're so cold, your teeth are chattering. C'mon. You can tell me everything over a mug of hot chocolate, and then we can decide what to do."

This time Nick told Cole everything. He didn't care if he was going to get in trouble for it. He needed to find Luther, and that meant telling Cole the whole story.

"How are your feet?" Cole asked, when Nick had finished talking.

Nick screwed up his face.

"They're burning like crazy, but I can feel my toes again, so at least I know I *have* feet."

"Good." Cole took a sip of his coffee.

"Cole?"

"Uh-huh?"

"How did you know where I was?"

"I followed you."

"You were spying on me?" Nick's eyes grew large.

"Hey, that's your hobby, not mine. No, it was a fluke. This morning I left home in such a rush that I forgot my briefcase. So I had to come back. That's when I saw you getting off the bus a few blocks from home. That didn't make sense – you should have been going to school. Then you took off in the wrong direction like you'd been shot from a cannon. So I followed you."

Nick lowered his eyes and toyed with his mug of hot chocolate. "I'm glad," he said quietly. In their silence, a country singer on the jukebox sang to a twanging guitar about broken hearts. "So, do you have a plan?" Nick asked finally.

"Well, not exactly, but I do have a couple of ideas."

"What?" Nick leaned forward, almost knocking

over his hot chocolate.

"Well, your Luther St. Cyr is no fool. He knows the dangers of taking to the road in weather like this. I'd be willing to bet that if he's leaving Andersonville, he's not doing it on foot."

"But what choice does he have? No one is going to give him a ride. Could he hop a train?"

"It's possible, but boxcars are just as cold as walking, only they're faster. No, I think Luther is probably going to take a bus."

"A bus?" Nick repeated in disbelief. "How could he? He hasn't got a cent."

"No, but he does have that gold pocket watch, and that has to be worth something. I think he'll pawn it for the bus fare."

Nick started to scramble out of the booth. "Well, what are we waiting for? We've got to catch him before he leaves."

Cole put a hand on Nick's arm.

"Relax." He looked at his watch. "He can't have gone anywhere yet – the pawn shops aren't open on Sundays, and they don't open today for another half hour. We have plenty of time to get to the bus station before Luther does. If we —"

The high-pitched beeping of Cole's pager stopped him in mid-sentence.

"Hang on a second," he said to Nick as he slid out of the booth. "It's the paper. They're probably wondering where I've gotten to. I'd better give them a call. I'll be right back."

When Cole returned, Nick had his jacket on and was spinning a spoon impatiently on the table.

"Can we go now?" He looked up at Cole anxiously.

"Yeah," Cole nodded, "but I'm afraid we're going to have to make a stop at the office first."

"Well, let's go then."

Cole left some money on the table. "Okay," he said, "but one thing first."

"What now?" Nick wailed.

"School," Cole announced, wagging a finger at Nick.

Was Cole going to drop him at school and go looking for Luther without him?

"We have to call your school before your school calls your mother."

Breathing a sigh of relief, Nick followed Cole to the pay phone.

"Good morning," Nick heard him say. "This is Cole Armstrong speaking. I'm just calling to let you know that my son, Nick Battle, won't be at school today … That's right … Yes, he …"

Nick didn't hear the rest. He was in shock. Cole had called him his *son*. Nick waited for the anger to roll over him, but it didn't come. Instead, he felt a trickle of pleasure, and a smile tugged at the corners of his mouth.

"Okay," Cole said, hanging up the receiver. "Shall we test our theory?" Then he noticed the smirk on Nick's face. "What's with you? You look like the cat who swallowed the canary."

"Do I?" Nick asked, unable to stop grinning. "I guess it just feels good to be warm again."

CHAPTER XVIII

T HE OFFICES OF *THE ANDERSONVILLE TIMES* WERE NO
more than ten minutes away, but Nick felt like it took
an hour to get there. The traffic was moving at a
crawl, and every light seemed stuck on red. They
even had to wait at a train crossing while exactly
thirty-seven railway cars rattled by – Nick counted
every one of them.

"Should I wait for you here?" Nick asked when they
finally pulled into the parking lot.

"No, come in. You'll go stir-crazy sitting in the car."

Cole's office was on the third floor and, rather than
wait for an elevator, they took the stairs. Nick could
barely keep up as Cole ran up the steps two at a time.

"What's the big deal?" he called after Cole. "What's
so important that you had to come back right now?"

"I'm not sure," Cole replied, not slowing his pace.
"The receptionist – that's who paged me – sounded
really flustered, but wouldn't say anything on the
phone except that *I* had to handle it – whatever *it* is.

All I can say is, it better be more than a jammed stapler."

As they pushed through the doors to the third floor, the flurry of activity made Nick's skin tingle. He'd only been here twice before, but each time it had been the same. Everyone was on the move. Telephones jangled insistently until they were answered by people already doing three other things. Computer keyboards clacked and printers printed non-stop, while shouts and laughter ran throughout the room.

Cole's office was off the reception area at the far end of the floor, so they had to weave their way through the maze of desks and reporters. Fascinated by all the goings-on, Nick soon fell behind. By the time he caught up, Cole had already reached the reception area and was trying to calm an obviously agitated young woman.

"... well, I couldn't let him just sit there, now could I? I mean, how would it look? This is a business office! What would people think if they saw a ... a ..."

"Now just slow down, Janice," Cole said. "I gather you asked him to leave?"

"Well, of course I asked him to leave, Mr. Armstrong. But he wouldn't. He refused! I mean —" Janice was nearly hyperventilating. "He just smiled and asked when you were expected. I told him I didn't know and suggested he come back later, but he just smiled again and said he'd wait. Then he picked up a magazine and sat down like … like … like he owned the place!"

"Then what happened? Take your time."

Janice shut her eyes and inhaled deeply to calm herself.

"I had been courteous," she began slowly, "but he wasn't paying any attention. So finally I raised my voice and told him in no uncertain terms that he would have to leave." Janice was speed-talking once more.

"And what did he say to that?" Cole asked patiently.

"Aargh!" Janice threw up her hands. "He smiled and, calm as can be, asked 'why?' Well, I'd had it, so I told him straight out that either he could leave the building under his own steam or I was calling security."

"I see," said Cole, "and how did he take your ultimatum?"

"He just kept on smiling and told me he didn't think I wanted to do that. I mean, really! There he was telling me what I should do! I figured he was just stalling but, anyhow, I asked him what he meant."

"And?"

"And he asked if I'd read today's paper." At this point, Janice looked away and continued apologetically, "Well, I haven't actually had a chance to read it yet, Mr. Armstrong. I was meaning to do it on my break."

Cole raised an eyebrow, but said nothing.

"So, anyway, he suggested I read the front page of the second section. Considering the nature of the article, he said he didn't think *The Times* would want him to go to the television station and tell them he'd been thrown out of here. So that's when I called you."

"Good, Janice. That was a wise thing to do." Cole glanced around the empty waiting room. "Where is he now?"

"Well, when I realized he wasn't going to leave until he'd talked to you, I suggested he wait in your office."

"Good idea," Cole smiled, and headed for his office.

"But he refused," Janice called after him.

Cole stopped, and looked at her quizzically. "So where is he?"

"The men's washroom," she replied. "But he's been there quite a while. Maybe he left after all. Should I buzz you if he comes back?"

"Please," was all Cole said. Then he turned and went into his office with Nick on his heels.

"What the heck was that all about?" Nick asked once the door was shut.

Cole tossed him a folded newspaper.

"Obviously you haven't read today's paper either."

Nick made a perfect catch. "Hey! I'm a kid. No

normal kid reads the paper every morning."

Cole was sorting through the mail on his desk and didn't bother to look up. "Everyone should read the paper, especially those people employed by it."

"Hello? Reality check." Nick waved his arms to catch Cole's eye. "You work for the paper — I don't."

Cole opened his desk drawer, removed an envelope and passed it to Nick.

"What's this?" Nick asked. The envelope had the newspaper's logo at the top left-hand corner. Nick's name was typed across the front.

"Open it."

Nick did. It contained a check from the newspaper made out to Nicholas Battle.

"It's a check," he said.

"For freelance services," Cole explained.

"What ser ..." For the first time, Nick noticed the amount of the check. His eyes grew wide. "Do you know how much money this is for? This is ..."

"I have an idea," Cole interrupted him. Then, taking pity on a totally bewildered Nick, Cole said, "The paper ... section two, front page."

Nick almost mangled the paper, but he finally found the page he was looking for. Already overloaded, Nick's brain couldn't quite understand what he was seeing. But the headline seemed familiar — *There's No Place Like Home* — and he recognized the photographs, too. Finally, everything clicked into place. He looked up at Cole in disbelief. It was his research report. On the front page of the second section of *The Andersonville Times*, for the entire city to read, was Nick's report about street people.

"You left it on the desk at home," Cole explained. "You'd said I could read it, so I did. I know I should have asked your permission, but I took a chance. I know how important this problem is to you and how you want to make a difference. Nick, your story is so powerful, I don't see how anyone could read it and not be moved. That's why I put it in the paper. I hope that's okay."

Nick was still speechless, so Cole continued.

"I don't know if you remember, but when you first came up with the idea for your report, I told you it would make a great topic for a series in the newspaper. That's what I intend to do – put together a series of articles by all sorts of people, not just regular reporters. Yours is the first one. In the lead-in to your report, I've explained that. Otherwise, I haven't changed a word. Well, I did touch up the grammar a bit. And the byline is yours. See? Your name, right there." Cole smiled and Nick looked back at the article.

The intercom on Cole's desk buzzed, and Janice announced in a snooty tone, "Luther St. Cyr to see you, sir."

KRISTIN BUTCHER

Nick's head snapped up and he and Cole stared at each other.

"Mr. Armstrong? Mr. Armstrong?" Janice repeated. "Are you there?"

Cole cleared his throat. "Yes, Janice. Please show Mr. St. Cyr in."

In answer to the expression on Nick's face, Cole said, "I'm as surprised as you are. When Janice said a bum was here, I just assumed it was someone from the streets ... because of your story. I certainly didn't think it was Luther."

Too much had happened too quickly, and Nick couldn't make sense of any of it. His feelings were all muddled up with his thoughts. Had the receptionist really announced Luther or was that just his mind playing tricks on him? No, it had to be real. Cole had heard it, too. But what was Luther doing here? It didn't make sense. Nothing made sense.

Cole met Luther at the door and, after the introductions, led him to a seat beside Nick. It was Luther all right, but his hair was wet and tied back from his face. His cheeks were rosy and his skin shone. He had a different smell about him too, a soapy smell, and Nick realized why Luther had been in the washroom for so long. He wanted to reach out and touch Luther — just to make sure Luther was really there, sitting in Cole's office — but he didn't.

For his part, Luther acted as if it was a normal,

156

everyday morning. He nodded toward the newspaper Nick was holding.

"Nice piece of work," he said.

"Luther, what are you doing here?" Nick hadn't intended to be so blunt, but the morning had taken its toll, and he needed answers.

"So much for small talk," Luther frowned. "Considering it's a school day, I might well ask you the same thing."

"I'm here because of you ... sort of," Nick started strong but finished lamely.

"And I'm here because of you ... sort of," Luther echoed.

"I thought you were here to see Cole," Nick countered suspiciously.

"I am. If you had listened, you would have heard me say I was here *because* of you. I didn't say I was here to *see* you."

"Oh," Nick mumbled.

Luther turned to Cole.

"A pretty good kid you have here. He has a tendency to jump to conclusions, but once he learns to listen, he should be fine."

Cole smiled and nodded. "We like him. He can be a little hotheaded, but his heart's in the right place. I think he's even developing a nose for news."

Luther sighed heavily. "That he is ... which is precisely what brings me here."

Cole leaned back in his chair and prepared to listen.

"I'm sure by now," Luther began, "Nick has told you about me." Cole nodded and Luther continued. "Though I never asked him to keep our friendship a secret, Nick sensed my need for privacy, and I know he wouldn't have said anything ever, if circumstances hadn't forced him to. That's a lot of pressure to put on a boy. Looking back, I can see how selfish I've been, but then hindsight is twenty-twenty, isn't it? Nick has been the spark I needed in my life. I guess I was so pleased to have his company and conversation that I didn't think about what effect the situation was having on him. Of course, I had no idea he knew so much about me, about my past."

Luther paused and looked at Nick, who was staring at his lap.

"I also didn't know anything about this article." Luther pointed to the newspaper. "I meant what I said earlier – it's an amazing piece of writing. Such insight and understanding are rare in most adults, but for a kid ..." Luther broke off and shook his head. "The world could use more Nick Battles. He puts the rest of us to shame – especially me."

Luther paused again. Then he slapped his knees, and his voice, which had faded to a near whisper, boomed out anew. "But I intend to change all that. Mr. Armstrong ..."

"Call me Cole, please," Cole said.

"Cole. In the lead-in to Nick's article, you indicated your intention to create a series of articles about people who live on the streets."

"That's right," Cole nodded.

"Well, I realize that nothing could have more impact than Nick's story ... but if you're interested, I'd like to contribute an article of my own to your series – a firsthand account about surviving on the streets. In ten years I've experienced a lot. I could tell your readers how I got there, how I survived and the way it's changed my life. I'm not a journalist, but I think I could do this ... if you're interested, that is. If it's not what you had in mind, I understand and apologize ..."

"I'm very interested," Cole said. "Firsthand experience is exactly what I'm looking for. But ten years on the street? We'll need two or three articles. Of course, the paper will provide you with the use of a desk and a computer." Nick had been sitting quietly the whole time, and Cole suddenly seemed to notice him. "But I'm getting ahead of myself."

He cleared his throat and straightened some papers on his desk. "We can work out all those details in good time." He smiled warmly at Luther. "I'd just like to say how pleased and honored I am to meet you at last. I really hope we get to know each other better." Then he glanced at his watch. "Look at the time. The morning's just flying by. Before we talk money and plan this series, I could use some coffee. How about you, Luther?"

Luther nodded. "I'd like that. Thank you."

"Good." Cole rubbed his hands together and headed for the door. "I shouldn't be too long."

Nick knew that Cole had left so Nick and Luther could talk privately. But now that they were alone, he didn't know what to say. It wasn't that he didn't want to talk to Luther, but he felt awkward and a bit shy.

"Did you get my note?" Luther asked.

Nick's eyes reflected the pain he'd felt earlier that morning at the McIntyre mansion. "Luther, I was so afraid. I thought you were running away again."

"So did I." Luther shook his head and almost chuckled. "After you left me on Saturday, I wasn't thinking too clearly. I'd kept those memories locked away for a long time, Nick. When you brought them out, I wasn't ready to face them. They were too much.

"That night I just kind of ran on automatic pilot," Luther continued. "My body had to fend for itself, because my mind wasn't there. I don't even remember most of what happened. I do remember that it took me a while to get moving. I knew it was too cold to stay in the house, so I headed for the Beacon Mission. But it was very late when I got there, and it was full. I think I spent most of the night on the move, trying to find a warm place – a heated bus shelter, a laundromat, a gas station washroom. It's only ever good for a few minutes, you know – before somebody boots you out.

"Anyway, by morning I was thinking more clearly. At least, I thought I was. I realized I couldn't stay in Andersonville any longer. You had discovered my identity; I wasn't safe anymore."

"Are you still leaving?" Nick asked anxiously.

"Just listen," Luther said, and Nick fell silent once more. "That day – yesterday – I went back to the McIntyre place and packed." Luther laughed. "Even to me, that sounds absurd. Anyway, there were a couple of things I didn't want to leave behind, so I went to pick them up. That's when I wrote you the note. I didn't want you worrying or blaming yourself. Then, late yesterday afternoon I went back to the Beacon Mission. I wanted to make sure I got a bed. I needed a good night's sleep, because I was planning to hit the road in the morning. The funny thing is that I got a bed all right, but I still didn't get any sleep. Last night the temperature hit a record low, and the Mission didn't turn anyone away. People were sleeping all over the place – in the halls, on the tables, everywhere. If the fire marshall had shown up, the Mission would have been closed down.

"I had to face it – the difference between me and almost everyone else there was that I had a choice. I was using the streets as an escape, a hideout. For most of the other people there, there was no choice – the Mission was the only thing they had left. All I kept thinking was that I was taking up space that someone else needed more than me."

Nick was shocked. "But you said no one was turned away last night – they would have frozen to death."

"That's true. But if there had been a fire, there's no way those people would have escaped. The Mission is just too small to meet the demand."

Nick looked at the envelope in his hand.

"Would this help?" he asked.

"What is it?"

"A check from the paper, for my story. I know it's not much for a problem this big."

Luther placed a hand on Nick's shoulder.

"Oh, Nick ... yes, your check would help. Every little bit helps. That's what people need to realize. The Great Wall of China is 1500 miles long – it can be seen from outer space – but it was built one stone at a time."

Nick changed the subject. "Are you still leaving?"

Luther sighed. "You just don't quit, do you? You're like a puppy tugging at my pant leg."

"Well, are you?" Nick's hopes were up, and he had to know.

"After last night at the Mission, I was more

determined than ever to move on, but it was so cold. I was afraid to start walking. I'd freeze before I made it to the city limits."

"Cole thought you might pawn your watch so you could take the bus," Nick said without thinking.

Luther scowled. "How does Cole know about my watch? For that matter, how do you know about it?"

There had been too many secrets.

"You left your room unlocked one day and I snooped. I'm sorry. It was wrong."

"Yes, it was. But it doesn't matter now. What's done is done, and we can't undo it by wishing. Believe me, I've tried." He paused. "You know, Cole is a pretty smart man. You could learn a lot from him. In any event, I decided I would wait until ten o'clock. If it didn't start to warm up by then, I was going to sell my watch. In the meantime, I thought I might as well catch up on the news. There's a fellow who reads his morning paper over coffee at a doughnut shop I know. When he's done, he tosses it into a litter container outside. I think he realized that I dig it out after he's gone, because lately he's taken to leaving the paper on a bench instead. Anyway, I saw your story. I was flabbergasted! No, that's an understatement. I was … I was … I don't know what I was! You had done something so important, and I was so proud of you."

Luther sniffed and cleared his throat before continuing.

"At the same time, I thought, I couldn't get away from you. I'd pushed you out of my mind, yet there you were, right under my nose, popping up like you always do when I least expect it." Luther stopped and smiled to himself. "That's when it hit me, like a two-by-four right between the eyes! It wasn't you I was running from. It was myself."

"Luther, I don't get it. You can't run away from yourself."

Luther sighed. "Why is it that a twelve year old can see what a grown man can't?" he asked of the ceiling. Then he turned to Nick. "It took me ten years – and your help – to figure that out. When my family died, I didn't know how I could go on. There didn't seem to be anything left to live for. So I stopped living. Oh, I didn't kill myself. I just ran away from my life. I didn't plan to live on the streets, but when I found myself there, I accepted it. Street life took all my thinking, all my wits just to survive. I didn't have to think about what I'd lost ... until you came along."

Luther inhaled deeply. "You wouldn't let me be. You were so curious about everything ... so enthusiastic, so righteous! You made me remember what living was all about. You made me think again, feel again ... care again."

"I did that?" Nick asked, incredulous.

Luther laughed at him. "That and a lot more. For one thing, you're doing something to help the people on the streets – the ones who have no choice. You've made me realize that I need to help too. If Cole wants my story about street life, that's a start. After that ..." he shrugged, "who knows. We'll have to see. To tell you the truth, I don't really know how to begin."

"I do!" The words were out almost before Luther had finished his sentence. "I know what you should do."

Nick was obviously scheming again, and Luther eyed him suspiciously.

"And what might that be?"

"Publish it – that last book you wrote for your son. Ms. Johnson still has it." Nick waited for Luther's reaction.

A shadow fell across Luther's features. He was obviously remembering. Then he looked at Nick solemnly and said, "Strange you should bring that up. I've been thinking about it myself – a lot. All these years, that book has haunted me. I blamed it for the accident. It had cost me my family – my life. And I hated it. But I couldn't bring myself to destroy it. I gave it to Ms. Johnson instead." Luther was wringing his hands and his voice was shaking. "I'd written it for my son. Everything in it was for Mathew – it *was* Mathew. How could I destroy it? All

I could do was walk away from it."

He took a deep breath before he continued. "All this time, I've pushed it to the back of my mind. I didn't want to think about it – I *couldn't* think about it – until now. I can't change what happened. I can't go back." He paused again. "But as long as I'm dragging the past with me, I can't go forward either. I have to let it go – not just Stefanie and Mathew. I have to let go of myself – at least, of the man I was then. I have to get free of that ghost."

He shrugged. "Maybe publishing that last book is a way of laying the past to rest once and for all. Then I can go on to do something else – to *be* someone else."

Nick realized that Luther's hurt would probably never completely go away. He'd just get better at living with it.

"You know," Nick said quietly, "the money from your book could sure help the street people."

The lines in Luther's face seemed to relax. Nick took it as an encouraging sign and pushed on more eagerly. "I think you should call Ms. Johnson – before you change your mind."

Just then, Cole returned with the coffee. "Oh, oh," he said. "That sounds like something I don't want to know anything about."

"You're a wise man," Luther said, but Nick broke in.

"Luther's gonna publish that book. You know,

Cole," he was hopping up and down he was so excited, "the one Ms. Johnson still has. He's gonna phone right now and tell her."

"Now, just hold on, Nick. I didn't say I would — not for sure. Besides, long distance calls cost money, which I don't have at the moment," Luther objected. "I'll write to her."

"The paper will pay for the call. Won't it, Cole?" Nick didn't notice Cole choke on his coffee. "It's good publicity. The money from the book is going to help the street people, and the paper will get credit for rediscovering a famous author. Right, Cole?"

"Oh, sure," agreed Cole, recovering from his coughing spell. "Obviously, you have everything worked out. But just in case the paper doesn't see it all your way, be prepared to have it deducted from your allowance."

Nick's mouth fell open and both men laughed.

"I'm kidding, I'm kidding!" Cole chuckled. "A long distance call is not a problem."

Nick turned to Luther and said smugly, "See, no problem."

"Right," Luther groaned. "I give up." Then he turned to Cole. "Can I please use your phone?"

Nick's eyes grew wide, and a smile spread across his face.

"*May* I use your phone," he gleefully corrected Luther.

Luther winced and his eyes narrowed, but there was a definite twinkle in them as he conceded, "*May I use your phone, Cole?*"

But Nick was already placing the receiver in Luther's hand.